GET THE NEXT BOOK IN THIS SERIES FREE

Sign up for the no-spam newsletter and get DAWN OF DREAMS.

Details can be found at the end of BREACH.

BREACH

BRONWYN LEROUX

CHAPTER ONE

It's happening again. There's nothing I can do to stop it. My tongue is a lump of clay in my mouth, incapable of movement, let alone speech. Any second now, perspiration will bead and trickle down my back. *I'm suffocating!* Sucking in a deep breath, my head clears somewhat. *How is it I'm fearless in battle but incapable of this simple task?*

In the rapidly dwindling light, Ceena's eyelids flutter as she glances down, her long, thick lashes almost touching her face. I'm ashamed to realize she is giving me time. Her eyes drop to her pretty feet. Moving a shapely leg forward, she scratches a pattern in the soft dirt with her toes. As she leans forward to inspect her design, a strand of glossy black hair falls over her face. Gracefully, she reaches up and tucks it behind her ear. Then, as if sensing my eyes on her, she looks up, her eyes catching and holding mine.

My breath hitches again. Suddenly, I'm the rabbit that scuttled away this morning when I went to check my snares. Except the rabbit evaded the trap I had set. I'm caught and there's no escape.

Ceena blinks, her warm brown eyes filling with concern. "Aiken?"

I have to say something. Anything. "Yes?"

Really, that's all I can manage? Yes? I sound like an idiot.

Ceena smiles. "Is there something you want?"

The lilt in her voice tells me she knows there is. My mind scrambles. *Why did I come here?* For a second, my brain is a blank slate. Then in a rush it comes back to me. I'm here to ask Ceena to attend the Harvest Festival with me. At the exact moment I remember, every limb seizes up again, and I begin hyperventilating. If I don't breathe, I am going to pass out. I open my mouth and gulp down air.

Alarmed, Ceena puts her hand on my arm. "Aiken, what's wrong?"

The contact is shocking. I leap back, then blush, mortified. *How am I bungling this so thoroughly?* Aiming to reassure Ceena, I croak, "I'll be okay."

I doubt my face supports the lie. This is not going the way it's supposed to. Again. Three years have passed since I'd first entertained the idea of asking Ceena to the Festival. I dreamed about it for two years and did nothing about it last year. This year, I decided it was time to man up. Today's the first time I've gathered enough courage to actually approach Ceena. But as usual, my wits have deserted me, and I'm an incoherent dolt when she's right in front of me. *I have to go.*

"Sorry," I mumble, twisting my bracelet around my wrist. "There's something I have to do."

I bolt. As soon as the closest building shields me from view, I stop, lean over and put my hands on my knees. Even dragging in lungfuls of air, it takes more than a few seconds to regain my composure. Shaking my head, I stand. *How can talking to a girl turn me into such a dunce? More disconcerting, why is it that this only happens with Ceena? I have no problems talking to the other women in the enclave.*

Grunting my irritation, I stomp back to my home. I crash through the door and glare at the interior: a large, single room with a fireplace. When the men of the village helped me build it, we left space to the side for a kitchen and washroom, things only added when a man gets married. Something that makes me think of Ceena again. I hiss. I made a total fool of myself today. *Will I ever be able to face her again?*

Morosely, my eyes wander over the four pieces of furniture I possess: a bed, a medium-sized table heaped with weapons and the tools of my trade, the single accompanying chair, and a chest topped with a washstand. My gaze lingers on the chest. It holds not only my clothes but also the one sentimental keepsake I allowed myself back when . . . Another event I prefer not to dwell on. The room's only redeeming feature is the fireplace and—*Oh no! The gathering!*

A trickle of my earlier excitement bubbles up. Rumor over dinner was that that the council planned on sharing a tale tonight that hasn't been heard in over a generation. That in itself is remarkable. Such stories are rare, usually because they have no lesson. Occasionally, though, some dark element makes them taboo. Judging by the general air of agitation in the village tonight, I'm guessing this story is the latter. Something that appeals to my over-developed sense of adventure.

I back out of my house and turn toward the meeting hall. When I encounter no one else along the way, I pick up the pace. By the time I rush into the hall, I'm dismayed to find almost everyone already there. Biting back a curse, I search for a spot near the fire where I won't miss a word.

I find Malthasus, my so-called best friend. I start in his direction before stopping short, not bothering to hide my disgust. He wouldn't notice. Did I really expect that he would have saved a place for me? Why bother when he can have two of the enclave's most beautiful women on either side of him instead!

I veer away, hoping to avoid Malthasus's attention. I loathe being an afterthought. Squeezing past the group of women gossiping in the corner, I apologize as I brush against them. Theoretically, not my fault that I touched them, as this building has so little space around the fire. But I practice the lessons of etiquette that were drilled into me. The women barely notice my intrusion, their conversation not even stuttering. Clearly, they aren't worried about me telling anyone what they were discussing. *Does that mean that I should've said they were gossiping? Probably not.*

Sighing, I reach the tiny space I hoped to secure. I squeeze between two of the larger villagers and sink down, elbowing a larger area for myself. Ignoring their glares, I survey the room. I'm further from the council than I wanted to be.

My eyes are drawn to Maliki, our enclave's seer. His clothes are a primal blend of animal skins, some decorated with painted markings that mean things I haven't bothered to memorize. Clicking around his neck is an odd assortment of teeth, stones and claws, held together by a thin leather cord. Add the colorful feathers he likes to adorn himself with, and he looks like something out of legend himself. That's when I notice the tightness around his eyes. The thin line he's drawn his lips into. The way his hands keep picking at his necklace. Is he nervous?

As though his agitation is contagious, I see signs of it in the council members on either side of him. Then in those further away. *What in the world is going on? Why are they all so tense? It's just a story. Same as every other night. Or is there something about this particular story that's making them unhinged?*

Movement to their right draws my attention, and my breathing stalls. Ceena weaves toward Racella. They've been friends practically since they were born. Ceena's graceful movements make it impossible for me to avert my eyes, her willowy body gliding around the others already gathered. Her smile as Racella acknowledges her makes me realize I'm about to pass out from holding my breath. I slurp in air so loudly that the man next to me turns and stares. I stare right back until he shifts his attention back to his companion.

That suits me just fine. Of their own volition, my eyes find Ceena again. She's now seated next to Racella, and their heads are close together as they share a whispered conversation. I wonder if Ceena's telling her about my bizarre behavior.

Those thoughts fizzle and die as I absorb the details I was too addled to notice earlier. Her dark hair is in its usual loose knot at the nape of her neck. But does it look less sleek than usual? Like Ceena tried to run her hands through it before remembering it was up?

Her hands move animatedly as she talks, and I notice the rings she wears. Silver with hints of the blue stones that can be found in this area. The blue stones match Ceena's pale blue shift which is adorned with bright red ribbons. The colors suit her, warming her bronze skin and lighting her caramel eyes. I groan inwardly. *Admiring her from afar has to stop. I have to stop making excuses. If only I didn't lose my tongue every time I stood in front of her, I might make some progress.*

"Welcome."

Breiden's deep voice cuts through the chatter. Conversations close respectfully as the enclave settles in for the evening's story. Every face around me reflects the same excitement I feel. Tonight's story is going to be a doozy.

Wriggling, I make myself more comfortable. I'm delighted it's Breiden telling the story. His baritone voice carries the perfect tone to convey a tale with the weight this one apparently has. More importantly, his voice is far louder than the others, and that means I won't miss a word. I settle back to listen.

More than an hour after the story ends, I am still sitting there, dazed. *Surely this tale can't be true. Can it?* I contemplate the story for the umpteenth time. My earlier assessment of "dark elements" was an understatement. This tale was so bleak, it completely drained the life out of the party that typically follows the telling. Most villagers scurried off as soon as the story ended. Those remaining spoke in hushed tones, as though speaking normally would make the dire predictions a reality.

I skim through the highlights again. Breiden said this story was an ancient legend. So at some point in time, part(s) of the story probably happened. The trick is figuring out which parts are true and which parts have been added over time to add spice. However, this tale is so far-fetched, I'm convinced the entire tale is fantasy.

My mind continues sifting through the main elements. A family charged with passing the story along. A stone box. Spirited away centuries past. A box that can only be opened by someone predicted to be important to its purpose. Symbols that mysteriously appeared on the box as it was carried to its hiding place. Symbols that signified something dreadful would happen. And not a single word about what was inside. Or why it had to be hidden. There had to be something in the box. *Why would anyone hide an empty box?*

Lost in reflection, I remain seated, listening to the whispered conversations around me. It seems I'm not the only one with questions about what was in the box. Idly, I wonder what Ceena makes of all this. My eyes roam the hall, but I don't see her. She's gone.

Sighing, I rise to my feet. It will be another long day tomorrow. And no doubt, there will be more than enough time to dwell on these matters then.

CHAPTER TWO

The sun is vibrant, heating the earth even though it's barely past sunrise. Dew evaporates around me in a vaporous mist, slinking between the dark shapes of trees. I creep through the forest on silent feet. It wouldn't do to scare any game that might have eluded my snares. I finger my bow and the arrow held ready just in case.

Nearing the last snare, I'm pleased to see this one has the best prize of the day—an almost fully grown doe. This should brighten the mood in the village. Carefully, I approach. She struggles, her nostrils flaring as she catches my scent. Slowly, I bend and draw the knife from my boot, making soothing sounds as I approach. Her large eyes are rimmed white with her fear, and she bucks, trying to free herself as she senses what's coming. In one fluid motion, I close the gap, grip her head firmly, and run my knife across her neck. I keep a hand on her neck, crooning as she passes from this world.

It doesn't take long to sling her carcass over the carrying pole. Before I leave, I use the nearby stream to cleanse the area, washing away the blood and the stench of fear and death. I won't be able to use this area again for a while. I gather up the lines I used and loop them through my belt. Then I sling the pole over my shoulder and begin the long trip home.

As I trudge, I ponder last night's story. Again. It's been plaguing me all morning and I'm still no closer to answers. By the time I'm halfway back to the village, I've decided there's no point to torturing myself further. As though making that decision frees my spirit, I feel a song rise within me. I let it loose, and by the time the village appears, my mood is infinitely improved.

The joyful cries as the first women on the outskirts of the village see the deer add to my jubilation. They come running and gleefully relieve me of my burden. Taking not only the deer, but also the small animals, they rush away.

I'm left standing alone. For the briefest moment, the strangest sensation washes over me. It's as though I am the only person left in the village. Even the sounds of life so evident a moment ago have vanished.

An inexplicable mist swirls around me. Through the fog, I make out the ruins of homes. Beyond the homes, thick plumes of smoke rise from the forest, blackening the sky. Crumpled corpses surround me. Disoriented, I snatch my spear off my back, turning in a circle as I scan for the enemy. Panic rises in me. *What just happened?* I spin faster, my eyes scouring the thickening mist. A black shape swirls toward me.

"Aiken?"

I freeze. I know the voice. I blink, and the haze around me clears. Suddenly, the sun blazes to life around me again, and the chatter of children as they lead the goats out to pasture buzzes in my ears. But the chill hasn't left my bones. The empty echoes of a decimated village haunt me.

"Aiken!"

This time, the sharp tone can't be ignored. My eyes focus on Malthasus standing in front of me, his brow furrowed. "What?" I bark.

"Why are you waving your spear around like a lunatic?"

Malthasus's words register, and I stare at the spear I'm clutching. My eyes dart to the dirt, and I observe the circular pattern of my footprints. There's no doubt I drew my spear and searched for the perpetrator of the nightmare I just saw. *How is that possible? Sure, it's not the middle of the day, but I wasn't sleeping. How could I have seen what I just saw unless I was dreaming?*

"Fine, don't answer me then," Malthasus huffs, stalking off.

I chase after him, my mind still trying to wrap itself around my bizarre experience. "You didn't see anything strange?" I ask when I draw level with Malthasus.

He shoots me an incredulous stare. "You're joking, right?"

Knowing Malthasus, it's probably wiser if I keep this little "incident" to myself. He'd love something he could use to one-up me. It's something he's been striving for ever since I toppled him from his ranking as best warrior. I remain silent, keeping pace as we stride toward the training grounds.

It's only then that I remember that I still have all my hunting gear with me. Mercifully, we haven't reached the place yet where I'd have to branch off to head home, or he would begin to wonder. Then again, maybe not. Sometimes I doubt he thinks further than how best to braid his hair that day.

I glance at the golden braid running almost the entire length of his back. This and his pale blue eyes, like chips of ice off a frozen lake, are what set him apart from the rest of the enclave. It's also the cause of his insecurities. He's a product of an *Iquera*—an outsider—and a village woman. The upside is that his unique looks have the attention of every woman not only in our village, but for miles around. I wonder if it's worth it.

"See you at training," I say as I peel off the path toward my home.

He nods and carries on walking. *How is it that I consider him my best friend? We're not friends. Not really. We were. Once. When we were younger, and he wasn't threatened by me.*

Grunting away the usual irritation these thoughts bring, I open the door to my home and step inside. I sling my equipment onto the wooden table and flop into the chair, then drop my head back and take a moment to just rest and consider.

As I think of the eerie interlude I had a few moments ago, last night's story returns to haunt me. Didn't Breiden say the council members who had hidden the stone box had vanished? That no one knew what had happened to them? That couldn't be right. If they'd vanished, how did anyone know they'd successfully hidden the box? Then again, was there anything in the story that said the box *had* been hidden successfully?

Recalling the details, this was implied. Or it could just be the way Breiden told the story. But deep down, I don't think so. The council have been recounting these stories for centuries, and they have a rhythm to them. A pattern that allows them to only be told a certain way. This ensures that all the relevant details that should be included are included.

Why am I now trying to make connections between last night's story and what happened to me on the way home this morning? Ugh, I can't sit anymore. I need to work out my frustrations. Rising, I hurry out of my home and head for the training grounds. The perfect place to work up a sweat and forget about frivolous stories and events that have no answers.

The first person I notice is Tamaan, Ceena's brother. He's already hard at work, going through a complicated training routine with Herkin, one of our best instructors. I study Tamaan, amazed as always at the wealth of natural ability he displays. He might even be better than me—his training is certainly progressing faster than mine did. He'll be a full warrior in less than a year, potentially beating my record for youngest warrior. I smile. Good for him. He hasn't merely relied on his talent; he's put in the work, and this combined with his talent is paying off. Big time.

I tug my leather jerkin off, then my undershirt, reveling in the sun's warmth. The pervasive chill in my bones is fading. And when I pick up a training sword and begin my warm-ups, the motions banish the rest of the chill. Or possibly it's just because my mind is focused on something else that I no longer feel the fear running up and down my spine like crawlers.

A couple of hours later, I'm soaked in sweat. I put myself through a more intensive session today, and I can feel it. The last round with Malthasus went about as expected, with Malthasus too eager for the quick win to make beating him something I can feel was a real achievement. It's left me with the sour taste of dissatisfaction, and as I take a swig of water, I wonder if I should run another bout with someone else to clear it.

My eyes fall on Tamaan. Without really thinking it through, I lift my chin at him, a silent question as to whether he wants to go a round with me. His eyes light up, and he nods enthusiastically. I grin, feeling better already.

As we take our places, I study him. His eyes are correctly focused on the center of my body, where his peripheral vision can respond to threats from any direction. He's calm, not excited or panicked. And he's ready for whatever I decide to throw at him.

I push into Bear Claw stance, and Tamaan's sword glides sideways as he assumes Rock Ledge stance, an excellent defense. We set to. In seconds, I repeat my earlier thought that he will probably be a better fighter than I am. For now, I still have the advantage, and I press it to win the round.

We begin again and run through another four rounds to complete the usual five rounds of a bout. When we finish, I'm not surprised he won two of the five. If I'm being totally honest, it was pure luck (or experience) that prevented him from winning a third, which was hotly contested.

We step back and press our crossed arms over our chest in the traditional sign of respect to one another. The round of whoops and applause make me realize the rest of the men have stopped their own fights to watch. I glance at Tamaan, my opinion of him only improving as I notice him accepting the compliments humbly. He's not letting them go to his head like Malthasus would've.

No, I'm not going there. I just got the foul taste of him out of my mouth. I grin at Tamaan. "It won't be long before you're beating me. Keep up the good work."

He almost glows at the words. I have to remind myself that Tamaan needs this encouragement more than ever now that he has no father to hand it out to him. I clap him on the back as I leave the training grounds for the day.

After a dip in the river to clean myself, I grab a quick lunch before spending the afternoon repairing and maintaining my hunting and fighting equipment. An hour before sundown, I head out into the forest again for the nightly check of my snares. The pickings are slim as expected, but I don't return empty-handed to the village once I've reset the snares.

The delicious aroma of roast deer wafts out to meet me before I've even crossed the bridge into the village and it makes my mouth water. I hurry home, eager to get rid of my trappings and grab some food from the communal cook fires.

I'm on my way to the dinner circle when I hear angry voices. I slow, trying to make out the words, but I'm too far away. I search for another route, not wanting to intrude on the argument as it will only delay my dinner. If the empty paths are any indication, the whole village is already there, meaning I should hurry.

As I round a building, the voices suddenly become clear, and I curse my bad luck at choosing the wrong alternative. Hurriedly, I step back into the shadows. Then I recognize Ceena's voice. I'm about to step forward, eager to come to her aid, when I realize that the person confronting her is Malthasus. I hesitate. *Should I intrude?*

Before I reach a decision, Ceena yells, "It's not your decision to make!"

She storms off. I watch, waiting to see if Malthasus will follow. He doesn't, but his stance worries me. I've seen it before, facing down marauding enclaves. It's the look of a man with murder on his mind. And hatred in his heart.

CHAPTER THREE

By the time I reach the dinner circle, most of the village is already congregated around the fire pits. The evening meal is about to get underway, and groups gather around the various platters on the tables. I slip into line behind Rioram and Rena, envying their easy companionship.

Rioram spots me. "Aiken, what's new?"

I shrug. "Not much. You?"

"I can't complain with the lovely Rena at my side." Rioram grins and takes Rena's hand in his own, planting a quick kiss on her cheek.

Rena's blush is impossible to miss. She gazes up at Rioram with adoring eyes. If only I could emulate Rioram. Relationships come so naturally to him. Maybe if I spent some time studying Rioram and Rena together, I might work it out.

Pushing thoughts of my inadequacies when it comes to Ceena aside, I say, "You can stay focused on Rena all you want as long as I can jump ahead of you and get my food!"

Chuckling, Rioram takes the hint and fills Rena's plate and then his own. Casually, he asks, "Are you actually going to invite someone to the Harvest Festival this year?"

I tense. Hadn't I just decided I wasn't going there? But Rioram doesn't know that. Trying to maintain his casual tone, I reply, "I have someone in mind."

Rioram raises an eyebrow. "Oh you have, have you? Who's the lucky lady?"

"Wouldn't you like to know!"

Rioram eyes me. "I take it you haven't actually asked her then?"

My grin falls away, and I grit my teeth. It takes all my self-control not to snap back. "Not yet. But I will."

For a moment, I think Roman's going to press the issue. Then he reconsiders and changes the subject. "I saw you brought in the dinner we're enjoying tonight. How's the hunting these days?"

I relax as the conversation takes a more familiar path. My angst is forgotten as others join us, and we swap details about our day, laughing and commiserating together. Finishing my meal, I search for Ceena and find she's still absent. *Did she eat early?* No, that's unlikely because dinner was only beginning when I arrived. I glance at my plate, wondering whether I should fix a plate and take it to her. Deciding it will be an excellent opportunity to have another shot at asking her to the festival, I rise and head to the food tables.

"Someone's hungry tonight," Rioram teases.

I ignore him and finish filling the plate before I comment. "Maybe I'll go eat this where I can have some peace and quiet."

Rioram smiles, but his speculative gaze as I leave makes me wonder whether he knows what I'm up to. *Now is not the time to second guess myself. In any way. I need to get this done.* I plod toward Ceena's home, hesitating when I finally reach it. Then taking a breath, I call, "Ceena?" I'm encouraged to hear movement inside. "Are you there?"

"What do you want, Aiken?" Ceena mumbles, her words faint behind the closed door.

"I noticed you weren't at dinner —" I begin.

The door flies open, and I stare at Ceena. Her hair has been freed from its knot and flows around her shoulders. She's changed into a dress that hugs her shapely form in all the right places. My mouth goes dry. *Oh no, not again. It was going so well.*

In a flash of inspiration, I realize why: because Ceena wasn't standing right in front of me! It's easier to talk to her when I can't see her. My gaze drops to the ground, and I try to imagine she's still behind her door.

"Well?" Ceena demands.

Flustered, my brain scrambles to remember what her question was. If I don't say something, I'll lose my opportunity again. My gaze shifts, and I notice the plate I'm holding. It reminds me why I'm here. She probably didn't hear the reply I gave earlier—or the part I managed to get out before she opened the door. And the plate gives me something to look at besides Ceena.

"I didn't see you at dinner so I brought you some food." When Ceena doesn't respond, I wonder if I should say something else. "I don't know what you like, so I brought a bit of everything," Suddenly aware that the plate is loaded with an astronomical amount of food, I rush on. "I don't really think you eat this much. . ." I drift off as I realize I'm being a klutz again.

Ceena saves me from myself. Her hand drifts into my line of vision as she takes the plate. "Thank you, Aiken. It was kind of you to think of me."

And that's when I make a fatal mistake. I look up at her, my eyes meeting hers. Any semblance of coherent thought flees. Her lovely face glows in the light flickering through the buildings from the central fires. The firelight bounces off her black hair, shiny and lustrous. Her large honey-brown eyes are liquid pools I can drown himself in. Her lips are red as pomegranate seeds and curved slightly upward as she smiles at me.

I'm terrified. But this is the moment. If I don't ask her now, I never will. The words came out in a rush. "Will you do me the honor of attending the Harvest Festival with me?"

Ceena's eyes widen in surprise. From her face, it's clear she wasn't expecting this. And now that I've said the words out loud, the words I practiced for so long, they sound stupid. *Have I just forever blighted myself in her sight?* Daring a glance at Ceena, I realize she's flustered. My heart plummets through my shoes and far into the earth beneath me. She's probably rummaging for a way to turn me down without hurting my feelings.

"Aiken, that's very kind of you to ask. But I have obligations. I'm sorry," Ceena mumbles.

Obligations? What is she talking about? The only person she has an obligation to, perhaps, is her younger brother. I haven't come this far to leave without answers.

"What sort of obligations?"

Ceena looks down at her foot, moving back and forth as she rolls a stone under it. She lifts a hand and tucks a strand of hair behind her ear.

I fidget. *Is this going to take long?*

Abruptly, Ceena stops moving the stone and shifts her weight, assuming a determined stance. "I'm sorry, I just can't go with you."

With that she dips her head and disappears inside her home, shutting the door quietly but firmly. I stare after her, scarcely able to believe she's gone. But she is. She rejected me. Numb, I turn away. I'm halfway back to my own home before I remember the plate of food. It wouldn't do to be wasteful. I stomp back to Ceena's home.

I'm surprised to find the door slightly ajar. My steps falter when I hear weeping. *Now what? Should I leave the food or leave her to her tears?* Compromising, I sneak up to the door, put the plate on the ground and slide it through her doorway. The crying jag continues, probably because her head's in her hands or her eyes are too full of tears to notice the offering. Either way, I can escape without having to confront Ceena again.

CHAPTER FOUR

The warm sun on my back the next morning does nothing to boost my spirits. I slash the line holding the rabbit. It's a tiny thing and not worth the time or effort it'll take to skin it. Freed, the rabbit darts off, its path haphazard. I watch it go, feeling the same way about how things have gone with Ceena—all over the place. If she didn't think I was a fool before, she's surely changed her mind.

I sag as I replay last night's rebuttal. Maybe she rejected me because she thinks I'm a fool. The sharp pain in my finger makes me curse. I blink, staring at the cut as it bleeds profusely. This is what comes of thinking of my deficiencies when it comes to Ceena rather than focusing on cutting the knot on the snare that refuses to release.

Growling, I grab my water skin and douse the cut. Now that I can see the wound, it's not that bad. Just a wakeup call to pay attention to what I'm doing. I pull the cloth I keep with me for just this reason out of my pack and wrap it tightly around my finger. Then I go back to resetting the snare, this time only thinking about what's right in front of me.

By the time I return to the village, it's late. My haul, mainly smaller animals and birds, is better than usual. This catch at least provides the option for some preserved meats. They'll be needed in the winter months when game is scarce.

Dropping my catch with the women tasked with food for today, I trudge home. For some reason, I'm dragging. I don't feel at all energized. Dumping my kit, I flop onto my bed and roll onto my back. I stare up at the ceiling, my mind numbed into nothingness. I'm tempted to just go back to sleep. But thinking of the ridicule I'd have to endure if I don't at least make an appearance at the training grounds, I force myself back onto my feet.

At my washbasin, I splash water over my face. Its icy fingers shock me, reviving me somewhat. Gasping, I repeat the process. A few rounds later, I'm feeling more like myself. But I can't shake the thundercloud that looms over me today.

Resigned, I head for the training grounds. I hear the shouting long before I get there. Not the usual cheers and jovial shouts—angry, confrontational sounds. I start running. As I burst free of the buildings on the side of the training grounds, I barge into the gathered crowd and shove my way through to reach the front.

Malthasus and Tamaan face off. Malthasus yells at the boy, his hands jerking in agitation. By contrast, Tamaan merely stands there, taking Malthasus's anger in stride.

"What's happening?" I ask Jashay, one of the other warriors standing in the circle that's formed around Malthasus and Tamaan.

"Tamaan refused to spar with Malthasus," Jashay answers, his attention on the two men.

I blink. *Really? That's what this is about? Tamaan refusing to go a round with Malthasus?* "That's all? Nothing else happened?" I press Jashay.

"Not that I know of," Jashay admits. "But Herkin and I were in the middle of a bout when they started up."

I turn back to the two antagonists just in time to see Malthasus take a swing at Tamaan. Tamaan ducks away, avoiding the blow, and Malthasus's face reddens. He lumbers toward Tamaan and takes another swipe. Tamaan dances away a second time. Malthasus's face is going from red to purple. I'm familiar with his rage. If someone doesn't intervene, this will end badly. I dash forward, placing myself between Malthasus and Tamaan.

"Out of the way, Aiken!" Malthasus roars.

"No," I answer quietly. Malthasus is going to make a fool of himself if I let this continue, and I'd rather endure his anger now than his ranting about his humiliation later. Malthasus steps forward, teeth bared and fists clenched. If he were taller, he might've been imposing.

"Step aside. This isn't your concern," Malthasus snaps.

"Allow us to resolve this on our own," Tamaan contends from behind me, his voice surprisingly controlled.

"What did Tamaan do to make you so angry?" I ask, ignoring them both. The easiest way to get Malthasus to back down is to make him think about what he's doing. If I can do that, his sense of self-preservation will kick in.

Malthasus stops. He frowns as though trying to remember, and then he smiles. "The louse insulted me."

I stare at him skeptically, That doesn't sound like Tamaan. He's too smart to malign someone he knows can probably best him in a fight. "How?"

"He refused to spar with me," Malthasus says, as though this makes him a hero.

"That's all?"

Malthasus glares at me, then abruptly deflates. His transformation as he actually starts thinking about his behavior is fascinating. Finally, he blusters, "It was the way he said it."

I only raise an eyebrow. With a snarl, Malthasus whirls away. That's when he notices the gathered crowd.

"What are all of you looking at?" Malthasus yells. His voice is enough of a catalyst to get the villagers moving on to more productive tasks. Malthasus glowers at them as they leave, then stomps off after them.

I turn my attention to Tamaan. "Are you alright?"

"You didn't need to rescue me. I was doing just fine on my own!"

His vehemence startles me. I'm not sure what to make of it. "I'm sorry. I intervened more for Malthasus's sake than yours."

"That's not how it looks to the rest of the village!" Tamaan storms off.

I'm left standing there, bewildered. Tamaan is usually one of the most level-headed young men in the village. In a moment of insight, I suddenly wonder if this has something to do with his sister. My mind races as it makes another connection. *Could this be why Ceena and Malthasus were having their little altercation?*

I really can't stand not knowing what's happening. Too many events in the past few days have raised too many questions, most notably whatever it was that happened to me yesterday when I entered the village. If I don't start getting some answers, I'll go stir crazy.

This drives me to Ceena's home. Even if it's a subconscious action, I can't deny that it's time I faced my own demons. Perhaps it's all these factors combined that led to my lethargy this morning.

As I near Ceena's home, the familiar anxiety rises in my stomach. Telling myself I should approach this the same way I face down our enemies, I fight back my trepidation. It takes monumental effort, but I make it all the way to Ceena's door. Squaring my shoulders, I raise my hand and knock.

CHAPTER FIVE

Ceena opens the door so suddenly, I take an involuntary step back. *Why does she keep doing that? It's unnerving!* Then my attention is arrested by her appearance. Her hair, usually so well groomed, stands out around her head as though she's just woken up. The mussed hair isn't as alarming as the dark circles under her eyes. Or the red eyes, evidence she's been crying again.

"What's wrong?" I blurt, my earlier apprehension drowned by concern.

Ceena doesn't answer. She stares at me as though she's never seen me before. I'm about to reach for her when she blinks a few times and focus returns to her eyes. "Oh, it's you."

Was she expecting someone else? "Are you all right?" I repeat.

Ceena nods, but the fugue is back. Her eyes are clouded, and she gazes at me, unseeing. My concern becomes full-blown panic. Taking her gently by the arm, I lead her back into her home. She allows the prodding, neither complaining nor resisting.

Subconsciously, my eyes take in the room. It's neat and tidy with everything in its place, unlike my home where my belongings are scattered from one end to the other. I notice a chair with an embroidered cushion next to the sturdy table. Leading Ceena to the chair, I ease her into it. Then I bend down and sit on my haunches in front of her. Taking her hand in my own, I change the question. "Can you tell me what's wrong?"

Ceena's eyes drift before finding my face. It takes a while, but clarity returns. She manages a weak smile. With her free hand, she reaches up and touches my face. "Dear Aiken, always there for those who need him."

I'm distracted by that touch. Her hands bear the callouses of the hours spent working with the reeds and other materials she uses for her baskets and mats. Not soft hands by any stretch. But the tenderness of the touch tugs at me. Her words finally filter through. *What is she talking about?* I try again. "Ceena, you need to tell me what's going on."

Ceena inhales sharply and looks away. Even though her face is averted, I can see the war she's waging with herself. Her shoulders are stiff, her jaw set in a tight line, and a tiny muscle pulses in her neck, a sure sign of her agitation. The hand that touched my face so tenderly now rubs at the callouses on her fingers.

I wait. Impatience won't encourage her to share the burden. I'm rewarded when she finally sighs and faces me again. "If I tell you what's bothering me, do you promise not to tell anyone?" After a brief hesitation, she adds, "Or do anything stupid?"

It's my turn to hesitate. I don't like the idea of knowing what the problem is but not being able to do anything about it. On the other hand, my curiosity burns. I reason that I can find a way around this promise if I have to. I don't dwell on the deceit. I nod my agreement, eager to get to the bottom of what's troubling Ceena.

"You'd better take a seat," Ceena begins, indicating a nearby chair.

I oblige. She pauses, wringing her hands. I'm wondering if she's changed her mind. Then I notice her eyes. The color of warm honey just harvested from the comb. Rich, brown, and with a soft, golden glow. I'm so mesmerized by her eyes that I almost flinch when she begins speaking.

"There's no easy way to say this, so I'll just jump right in. Racella is pregnant."

"What?" The single word doesn't do justice to my shock.

"You heard right."

"Who's the father?"

"Malthasus."

I allow the information to sink in. *When did that happen? I always know when Malthasus is seeing someone. He's constantly bragging about his conquests. But I never heard a single word about Racella.* "Are you sure it's Malthasus?"

Ceena glares at me. "I think Racella would know who the father was."

"Yes," I stammer, "it's just that Malthasus never said anything about her."

"Are you saying Racella's lying? Or that I am?"

I stop and take a breath. If I don't put a filter between my mouth and my brain, I'm going to say something else to offend Ceena. And the angrier she gets, the less likely she'll share the rest of the story. Because, in my bones, I can feel there's more to this.

"I'm sorry it sounded that way. What I should have explained is that Malthasus can't help boasting about the women he's flirting with. Or the women he's interested in. He never said anything about Racella." I raise my hands to forestall Ceena's impending interruption. "That doesn't mean I don't believe you. Malthasus excels at self-preservation. Considering his actions weren't noble, it fits that he didn't make his intentions common knowledge when it came to Racella."

Ceena's mouth sets in a grim line. "Now that sounds more like the Malthasus I know."

I debate asking the question now rearing its head or allowing Ceena to continue without prompting. Studying my face, she preempts me. "Malthasus is refusing to acknowledge his responsibilities."

Even though I'm aware Malthasus isn't the most honorable person, this is a sucker punch. "What? The evidence will be there for everyone to see soon enough. How's he going to explain that?"

"Remember the nomadic traders that came through a few weeks ago?"

"He's going to blame them!" I recall another detail. One of their young men was particularly handsome. He had Malthasus in knots because he temporarily drew the women's interest away from Malthasus. "Not, not 'them.' Malthasus's going to say it was that attractive fellow, what was his name?"

"Sanjeen," Ceena supplies.

I nod. It fits. "Malthasus will create some lie about Sanjeen seducing Racella, Racella being too weak too resist, then being too ashamed to admit to her actions now that there's a consequence. He'll say Racella's using the pregnancy to force one of the most eligible men in the enclave to marry her."

Ceena's giggle is unexpected. I'm so focused on working through Malthasus's scheme that I wasn't paying attention to Ceena. I find her eyes twinkling with mischief.

"One of the most eligible men?" she sputters before erupting into a fresh round of giggles.

I'm relieved to see her carefree again. I've missed that glorious smile. I grin. "Well, we all know that's how *he* sees himself."

She only laughs all the more.

My smile fades as I realize this still doesn't explain things. "Is that why you were crying? Why you and Malthasus were arguing the other night?"

Ceena sobers. Her eyes narrow and glint dangerously. *Now what did I say?*

"You've been spying on me?"

My own eyes widen. "What? No! I was on my way to dinner when I almost ran into you and Malthasus squabbling."

"And you didn't think to make your presence known?"

Her voice is soft. Somehow, this is more menacing than if she'd been yelling. "I didn't think it was my place to interfere."

Ceena studies me. Then she sighs. It seems she's realized she's being unreasonable. "Yes, I was crying because I was upset about Racella. I was also crying because of the situation Malthasus's trying to coerce me into."

I lean forward This is what I've been waiting for. "Care to elaborate?"

Ceena raises her eyebrows, then lifts her eyes to the ceiling as her head weaves from side to side. It seems she's searching for inspiration. Then the words come tumbling out. "Malthasus has promised to at least provide for Racella and the baby if I agree to go to the Festival with him. How messed up is that?" Her expression changes from exasperation to anger. "That's not all. If I go the Festival with him, he's also promised to leave my brother alone."

The altercation between Malthasus and Tamaan suddenly makes sense. I say nothing though as I sense the crux of the matter has still not been reached. I don't have to wait long.

Ceena sighs. "But if I do go to the Festival with Malthasus, I know he's going to use that as justification for approaching the council for permission to marry me."

My world drops out from under me. If I wasn't sitting, I would've fallen. *Marry?* I feel my hopes being crushed like kernels of wheat at the mill.

"Well, say something," Ceena demands.

Choking my emotions, I set my face into what I hope is a blank mask. I muddle through the issues. "First off, Malthasus needs to take responsibility for his actions and not make everyone else pay for them. That's what he's doing trying to blackmail you into going to the Festival with him. He needs to step up and acknowledge what he did with Racella. If you go to the Festival with him, you're only condoning his bad behavior."

"But my brother. . ."

"Is his own man. He is quite capable of taking care of himself. Stop seeing him as your little brother that needs protection." Ceena opens her mouth to argue, and I give her the details of yesterday's confrontation between Malthasus and her brother. I'm gratified when she chooses not to argue after that. It allows me to continue.

"Like I said, Racella is Malthasus's problem. By attending the Festival with him, you're only allowing yourself to be a pawn in his game. You have the freedom to choose your own path. You don't have to do anything you don't want to. And if it sets your mind at ease, I'll train with Tamaan to speed up his proficiency. He already has a wealth of natural talent. It won't take much to get him to the point where he can more than stand his ground against Malthasus."

The gratitude on Ceena's face is almost more than I can bear. I stand and begin pacing the room, more as a means to not look at her than anything else. I stop in my tracks when she places a hand on my shoulder. I resist the shudder. I've wanted her touch for so long, the contact is almost surreal.

"Is that offer to go to the Festival with you still open?"

I close my eyes, glad Ceena is still behind me so she can't see the pain there. I don't want her coming to the Festival with me because she feels like she owes it to me. "No, I've put myself on patrol rotation."

Ceena immediately withdraws her hand. I hear her walk away. My shoulders tense up again. I almost regret the rebuttal. But I won't be the solution to all her problems. Especially not the problem of Malthasus approaching the council about marrying her. She'll have to fight that battle on her own. I hate second place, and I won't settle for it. If she really wants me, for who I am and not what I can do for her, then she'll have to make that plain. More than anything, I want her to *want* to go to the Festival with me.

At peace with my decision, I turn to leave. Ceena's at her work table, her back to me. I deliberately avoid studying her too closely. If she's upset, it will be impossible for me to not question myself. She needs time to think things through before rushing into a decision about me. I head for the door. "See you around."

I don't wait for a response. Outside, I sigh, relieved to be out of her home. It's only then that I realize I had an entire conversation with her. *Without* stuttering or stumbling around like I usually do. Walking away, I assess this.

By the time I reach my home, I've concluded the reason I was able to talk to her was because I'd removed her from the pedestal I'd put her on three years ago when I first decided to ask her to the Festival. Somehow, I made her more than a person. Seeing her so distraught today, I realized she was as mortal as I was. She has fears and aspirations of her own. All of which made her more human to me and thus more approachable. Ceena needed my protection, not my worship. I make a mental note to avoid making a similar mistake in the future. Putting people on pedestals only leads to problems. Feeling less burdened for the first time in days, I begin whistling as I gather my things for the evening's hunt.

CHAPTER SIX

The twig snapping under Tamaan's foot telegraphs his intent. I duck, avoiding the roundhouse kick. Darting under him, I push up with my fist and land a solid blow on his stomach. With a whoosh, the air leaves him, and he stumbles back, gasping.

I straighten. "That move would've produced a better result if you'd remembered that the placement of your feet will give you away."

Tamaan grunts acknowledgement. I turn and reach for my water skin as I wait for him to get his breath back. The water's deliciously cool, but there's not enough of it. I shake the empty water skin, trying to squeeze a few more drops out. It's no use. "We need more water. Let's talk while we walk."

Reaching for my over-shirt, hanging on a nearby branch, I sling it over my head before heading deeper into the forest. This particular part of the forest isn't as familiar to me as other areas. Probably because the hunting isn't especially productive here. I happened upon this clearing only a week ago and was reminded of it when thinking of a place I could spend time training Tamaan without the rest of the enclave knowing.

Strange that it has remained hidden for so long. Most other spots this secluded and close to home have been ferreted out and are favorites for romantic liaisons. I pick my way through the under-brush, careful not to disturb the vegetation. I'm pleased to hear Tamaan being just as cautious as me. After all, we don't want anyone else finding this place. A random thought strikes me. *How has the clearing remained free of vegetation without pruning?*

"I thought we were going to talk as we walked?" Tamaan says, breaking my line of thought.

"Yes," I reply before launching into an analysis of his attack and my counter-attack, pointing out areas where he could've altered his approach to be more effective. I'm so engrossed in analyzing things in my mind I almost fall into the pool.

It appears out of nowhere, and I check my bearings. How is it that within a week I find not one, but two areas I've never seen before? Or maybe they were here all along, and I just kept missing them by being slightly off-track? Deciding this must be the reason, I gaze at the pool.

It's breathtaking. From its deep azure hue, I'd guess the pool's deep. Rocks surround it on all sides, bright green moss growing on the shady, north facing sides. The sunlight, dipping into this little piece of heaven through the opening created by the lack of tree limbs overhead, is a shaft of pure gold. It reflects off the water, throwing shimmering light all around. I search for a water source, but don't find it.

"Did you know this was here?" Tamaan breathes next to me, his voice so full of awe as to be almost inaudible.

"No, I've never seen it before."

"Why are you frowning?" Tamaan asks.

I scratch my head. "If that's north," I say, pointing back in the direction we came from, "then that means the river that flows past the village should be there." I indicate, and Tamaan nods. "It follows then that the lake should be that way, and the beaver dam should be over there." I point as I go.

"So?"

"How does this pool fit into that picture? The river would have to take a serious turn to reach this part."

Tamaan shrugs. "Perhaps it's a side stream that feeds into the main river?"

I evaluate the comment, but however much I do the math, it still doesn't seem feasible. "Perhaps. Let's fill up our skins and get back to training."

I amble over to a section where the rocks allow easier access to the water. Clambering over the boulders, I'm amazed at how difficult they are to negotiate. Obstacles like this don't usually pose a problem for me. Determined, I pick my way across the rocks, even more surprised when I'm breathing heavily by the time I reach the boulder closest to the water. I bend down to fill my skin.

It happens so suddenly I almost don't realize I've slipped until the water's closing over my head. I kick with my feet, aiming to get back to the surface. But the water feels . . . wrong. There's nothing to push against. I kick harder. But I keep sinking.

Panic sets in. Everyone knows I hate water. Ever since I fell into the river as a kid when my guardians weren't attentive enough and I almost drowned. Thrashing my arms in addition to my legs, I try again. But some unseen force is dragging me down. I lift my head, watching as the trees rimming the pool fade to blackness. Then even the light that made the pool seem so inviting disappears.

My lungs are going to burst. I can feel the blood beating against my brain as it demands air. Black spots dance in front of my eyes. I can't hold out much longer. Vaguely, I wonder where Tamaan is. *Did he not see me fall in? Why isn't he here to save me?*

I can't help it. I open my mouth and draw in. . . air? It's not water. I'm not choking like I did the day I almost drowned. Tentatively, I try another breath. As my body accepts relief from the deprivation, it demands more air. Greedily, I gulp it down.

Only when the need is satiated do I notice my surroundings. Or the lack thereof. It's like I'm in some sort of void. No sound. No smell. Just me. In a pool of light that has no apparent source. And the blackness beyond. I take a few steps forward. The light moves with me. *What is this place?*

I remain where I am, my mind galloping as I consider my options.

Clearly, I was at the edge of the pool. Then I fell in—or was I pulled in? The more I deliberate that point, the more pervasive the chill in my bones gets. Yes, I was definitely pulled into the pool, then sucked down here. *How am I going to get back?*

I become aware of a new sensation. The reverberations quaking through my body. Like a small pulse beating in time to some ancient rhythm. It reminds me of the way my body feels when the drums are hit too hard. Yet there's no sound.

Slowly, I turn, inspecting my surroundings. Nothing's changed. I don't know why I expected it would. I half turn, but there it is. Again. The slight change in the rhythm thudding through me. *Did it just get a little louder?* I laugh, the sound muted in this strange place. Impossible that something I can't even hear could get louder. Then again. . . I test what happens when I turn away. Yes, the sound is definitely softer, the beating against my body not as intense. I turn back to where the rhythm was loudest and take a step forward. This time, the difference is unmistakable. I take another step, then another as the drumming through my body intensifies.

While there's no pain, the sensation is uncomfortable. Does that mean I should be walking away instead of toward whatever is causing this? Something glints in the darkness beyond the light. I tense. *A predator? No, it's not eyes. Something else.*

I creep forward. The light catches again. A blue spark. The thudding in my veins is now almost indistinguishable from that of my heart. Then the light exposes what it's hiding. I gasp.

CHAPTER SEVEN

Defying the void, it waits on a pedestal, exactly as it was described. Except no one said it was so ornate. The sapphires blaze with blue fire as the light envelops them. They adorn the lid and sides, every size and shape. An enclave's ransom.

I lick my lips. Suddenly, my mouth is too dry. The blood rushing through my ears too loud. My body doesn't feel like it can take much more abuse from whatever is beating against it. Maybe if I just touch it. . . *No!* I snatch back the hand that was reaching forward. *What am I thinking?* I start turning and have to catch myself as I overbalance.

Dumbfounded, I stare at my feet. I try lifting one foot. *Nope.* The other won't budge either. It's like someone spread gummy tree sap over the floor and stuck my feet into position. I laugh hysterically. *This can't be happening!*

Abruptly, it all stops. The pain, the inability to move, the sound that isn't a sound. The feeling that things are out of control. Too stunned to move, I just stand there. That's when I notice my hand resting on the stone box. Aghast, I wrench it away. The pain is even more unbearable, the beating against my body so intense I'm sure it's going to break bones. I slam my hand back onto the box. The world calms.

Okay, the box stops the insanity. I test my left foot. It moves freely. Taking two careful steps, I inch closer to the box and dare to place my other hand on it. When there aren't any fireworks, I figure it's safe. My fingers explore the fabled artifact. The obsidian stone between the gems is smooth and cool. By contrast, the honed edges of the cut gems will slice my finger off if I'm not careful. Curious, I inspect the lid.

Yes, the symbols are there. Just like the council described them in the story they told not even a week ago. What they didn't say is that the sapphires form part of the symbol, their edges neatly aligned with the etched edges of the carved symbol. *What does it all mean? Will anyone even believe me if I tell them I found the box? Can I take the box with me?*

Nervous, I grip the edges of the box. I try convince myself that the council never said anything about not touching the box. Or picking it up. A tiny voice in the back of my mind screams that they never said it was hidden in a pool either. *Only one way to find out.* Taking a deep breath, I yank the box off its pedestal.

It's like I've been thrust into a powerful waterfall. The water gushes around me, pummeling me from all sides. All I can think is that I am thankful I took that breath. The water presses against me. *No, it's pushing under me.* I'm being propelled upward. Then I'm flying through the air, yelling at the top of my lungs. Images of those rocks around the pool careen through my head.

Before I can focus my eyes and find those rocks, I hit the ground. Soft, mossy ground. No rocks. Dazed, I lie there for a moment, evaluating the state of my body. Nothing feels broken. Slowly, I sit up. The box is still clutched in my hands. My eyes roam further. *Where am I?*

"Aiken!"

Are my ears deceiving me? That sounds like Tamaan. No, I must be lucid because Tamaan comes sprinting through the trees, his face ashen.

"Are you alright?"

I nod, still too shaken to speak.

"You came flying out of that water like a dragon spat you out! I thought you'd be dead for sure."

33

When I only stare, he rushes closer and kneels down next to me. I know the moment he spots the box.

"Is that what I think it is?" Tamaan whispers.

"Yeah." I squeeze the single word out. But Tamaan's attention is centered on the box.

"Did you try and open it?"

Duh! I feel pretty dense right then. Wasn't I the one obsessing about what was inside the famed object? I dump the box on the ground between my legs, eager to get at the lid. But no matter how hard I pull, the lid doesn't budge. My fingers almost fall over each other as I try each side in turn. Still no result. The lid is jammed shut. I sigh as I lean back, defeated. *Well, of course the lid wasn't going to open! If it didn't open through that nightmare exit from the pool, it's unlikely my feeble attempts are going to make a difference.*

"Can I try?" Tamaan asks when he notices I've abandoned my efforts.

I shrug. "You can, but be forewarned that the box might do strange things when you touch it." Tamaan's hand immediately retracts.

"Like what?"

I outline my experiences in the pool. By the time I'm finished, Tamaan is gaping.

"All that happened while you were in the pool?"

"You don't believe me?"

"No, it's just that you were only in the water for about a second before you came flying back out."

I digest this tidbit. Another sigh escapes. *Well, that explains why Tamaan didn't dive in to save me.*

"What are we going to do with the box?"

Hmm, good question. "At this rate, I'm thinking of just throwing it back into the pool." I pick up the stone box. As I do, something rattles. "So there is something inside!" I shake the box.

"Don't do that." When I pause long enough to raise an eyebrow, he says, "Whatever's in there could break."

I'm suddenly irrationally, irrefutably, irritated. *Stupid box with its stupid puzzle!* I bound up and dash in the direction of the pool before

Tamaan can respond. I'm more than halfway there by the time Tamaan catches up.

"Hold up. You're not seriously going to throw it back into the pool?"

I don't bother to answer. I keep running. Five minutes later I screech to a stop. Tamaan crashes into me.

"What's wrong?"

"Shouldn't we have reached the pool by now?"

Tamaan considers. "Yeah. Did we go in the wrong direction?"

Somehow, I already know we're not going to find the pool. No matter how long we look or how much ground we cover. Reluctant to accept this, I hunt for the signs that tell me we've been here before. It doesn't take long to track the paths we've followed.

Although I speculated we wouldn't find the pool, I didn't expect to find we've been traveling in circles. When we arrive back at the same spot ten minutes later without encountering the pool, the confusion on Tamaan's face is almost comical. "You didn't really expect that we'd find it, did you?"

Tamaan lifts a hand and scratches his head. "No, I suppose not." He hesitates. "You still haven't answered my question. What are we going to do with the box?"

This time, I ponder the question. *Taking the box back to the council will only cause panic. Especially since the cautionary tale was shared so recently. I can't throw it back into a pool I can't find. Will the box do something weird to me if I leave it alone like it did when I was in the pool—or under the pool—or wherever I was? No, leaving the box here in the middle of nowhere is irresponsible. The box must be important. Why else would we have found it now?*

When I start laughing, Tamaan frowns. "What?"

"Here I am thinking we found the box. More like the box found us."

Tamaan grins. "True. I suppose we shouldn't abandon it then?"

I study him. *Why is he so worried about me disposing of the box?* "Something you're not telling me?"

Tamaan's face reddens. He tries to shrug it off. "I don't know. I mean, it's like the box—well, you know."

Okay, I'm confused. "No, I don't know. Tell me." If anything, Tamaan looks even more embarrassed. He runs a hand over the short, spiky hair on top of his head. Then he looks around as though the forest will provide inspiration. "Spit it out."

"Don't you feel, um, connected to the box?"

The statement is so unexpected, my jaw drops.

Tamaan rushes to explain. "Don't you feel like you were *supposed* to find it? Like the box *wants* you to hold it?"

Even as he says the words, his hand is reaching for the box again. This time, I don't stop him. If anything, I want to see if it affects him in any way. When nothing happens, I'm almost disappointed. Almost. I suppose I should be protecting Tamaan, considering he is still a minor in the enclave's eyes.

"Since you feel such a connection to it, how about you keep it?"

Tamaan's eyes bulge as he considers the implications.

I rush to correct any misconceptions he might have. "Not to keep forever. Just for a while. Until we figure out what to do with it. I don't think we should tell the council yet. But we clearly can't leave it here either."

Tamaan relaxes. Then I see concern flit over his face again.

"What now?"

"Do you think it will be safe to keep in our home? I mean, Ceena, I have to keep her safe."

Ceena! How could I have forgotten? Tamaan still lives with Ceena. I make a decision. "Alright, I'll keep it in my home then. But only until we know what to do with it. And just to be clear, I don't want you telling anyone we found it. Okay?"

"Yeah. I don't want anyone knowing we found it either. If they did, they'd want to see it, and then the fighting would start."

"What do you mean?"

"You don't think they'd want the wealth this box represents?"

He has a point. "Okay, we take it back, hide it away, and think about what to do with it." Tamaan nods his agreement. "Let's go. Or we'll be late for dinner, and we don't want people to start asking questions."

CHAPTER EIGHT

"Don't be angry with Tamaan," Ceena scolds. "I know my brother and I know when something's troubling him. I also know how to finagle it out of him!"

I'm scarcely able to believe she's the same sweet person I grew up with. When did she become the Mama Bear, all protective of her family and growling at everyone? I pace in an effort to calm down. Noticing my fists are still clenched in tight balls, I uncurl my fingers and shake my hands. *Why, oh why, couldn't Tamaan keep his mouth shut?*

I mentally count to ten before I speak. "So you know about the box. Are you going to tell the council?"

Ceena's gaze burns into my skull. Who knew honey could be so hot? Her eyes are almost golden. With a jolt, I realize she's speaking. "Pardon?"

"I said, what kind of idiot do you take me for?"

Well, there, she put me in my place, didn't she? I bite back the fresh anger. "I never thought you were an idiot. I'm simply trying to estab-lish what action you're considering taking."

"Why not ask that then? Would it be so difficult to say, 'Hey, Ceena, now that you know about the box, what do you think we should do about it?' instead of just assuming my first course of action will be to blab to everyone about it!"

I scrub a hand over my face. Honestly, I've never been good at discerning the finer points of communication. Maybe it stems from growing up without a family. Either way, Ceena thinks my approach was flawed, and I can't argue the point. Abruptly exhausted, I flop onto the nearest surface, then bounce up in alarm when I realize it's Ceena's bed. "Sorry," I mumble.

Out of the corner of my eye, I notice Ceena studying me. She must be wondering whether the apology was for my ineptness at communicating or sitting on her bed. I can almost see the argument raging in her head as to whether she should say more. Thankfully, she takes pity on me.

"Apology accepted." Her eyes drop to her hands, rubbing at the callouses there.

I recognize the movement for what it is—her uncertainty how to proceed. My turn to do some saving. "I guess we could hide the box here instead. You have way more hiding places." I gesture toward the many mats and baskets in her work area.

Ceena smiles hesitantly. "Don't you think that's the first place someone would look if they came here searching for something?"

"Fair point," I acknowledge with a smile of my own.

Her answering smile reaches her eyes this time. "Okay, so let's find a better place to hide it."

Tamaan interjects. I had forgotten he was here. "You two decide without me. I won't be able to keep that secret, and I don't want to."

He stalks out the room, and Ceena moves to rush after him. I step forward and place a hand on her arm. "Let him be. He already feels like he's let me down by spilling our secret to you. Don't remind him of that by telling him he can do this. Allow him to make his own decisions."

Ceena sighs as she backs down. "I suppose. He looks up to you, do you know that?"

And I'm uncomfortable again. Just when we were having a normal conversation, she brings something personal into it.

As if realizing this, Ceena hurries to add, "He's enjoying the time he's spending training with you."

I grab at the lifeline. "He's easy to teach. And he has a lot of natural talent."

"I'm sure he'd be encouraged to hear you say that." There's another strained silence. Then Ceena's face brightens. "Why don't we go find a hiding place for that thing?"

Yes, please! My reply when I give it is tempered so as not to show my eagerness to be free of this polite conversation. "Do you have any suggestions?"

Ceena's eyes sparkle. "How about the old caves?"

I gape. "You mean the ones with the painted foretelling?"

"Why not? It would give us the chance to see if there's a picture up there of the box. Also, no one goes there anymore. And the less visited a place is, the better the chances are that the box will stay hidden."

"I suppose it's a starting point."

"You don't seem that eager. Is there a problem?"

"You don't find that place creepy?"

Her giggle is infectious. I can't help the smile that cracks across my face. "Aiken, our enclave's greatest warrior, afraid of some old caves?"

I take the teasing in the spirit in which it's intended. "Who knew? He's probably scared of the dark too!"

Ceena's giggles morph into laughter, and soon I'm laughing with her. This is more like it used to be. When we could talk for hours as friends growing up together. Determined to maintain this atmosphere, I don't stretch out my hand toward her as I say, "Shall we?"

Reaching for a basket, Ceena says, "Not without this."

I frown.

"To disguise the box. Is this basket big enough?" I nod, and she tosses some mats into the basket. "We'll put these over the top."

Leaving five minutes apart, we sneak off to my home using separate paths. Despite leaving after Ceena, I'm already waiting by the time Ceena opens my door.

She grins. "Did anyone see you?"

I laugh. "It would be stranger for you to be entering my home than me. The more appropriate question is whether anyone saw you?"

Tossing her glossy hair, she says, "Who would be interested in what I'm up to? Where's the box?"

I slide it from its hiding place. Ceena gasps, and I grin.

"Wow! Tamaan said it was beautiful. I didn't think it was this spectacular!"

When Ceena reaches for the box, I hand it over. The sapphires flash in the dim light, bouncing blue light onto Ceena's face. Her wonder is something to behold: her eyes are wide, her mouth slightly open. The stone's blue hues make her eyes a richer brown, her lips a deeper red. My eyes are drawn to that mouth. Her lips are soft and full, shaped in a small "o." I realize I'm staring. Turning to hide my embarrassment, I pick up the basket she dropped.

"Let's hide the box and be on our way," I mutter.

Reluctantly, she places the box in the basket and covers it with the mats. When she reaches for the handle, I maintain my hold.

Ceena rolls her eyes. "It'll look odd for you to be carrying a basket."

She's right, of course. I hand it over. "Okay, you go first and I'll follow at a discreet distance. I'll meet you at the twisted pine on the other side of the river."

With a furtive check outside, Ceena slips out. I wait for a few minutes before following her. No one's around to watch as I make my way out of the village. I'm beginning to wonder where everyone is until I reach the fields surrounding our village. Fertile and green, I see our people ducking through the corn and wheat stalks as they check on the crop. Squelching the guilt that I'm not there helping, I slide into the nearby forest and make my way to the twisted pine.

As I approach, I grin when I notice Ceena jumping at every sound. I feel like a hero when she sees me. Her shoulders sag with relief and her lips curve into a broad smile. *Pity she didn't run to me and throw her arms around me.* Shaking off my idiot daydreams, I ask, "Any trouble getting here?"

"No. But I did feel bad about not helping with the crops."

I grimace. "Me too. Let's hurry and hide this, then we join them before they notice we aren't there."

She nods, and we set off. It should only take about thirty minutes to reach the caves, but the path is so overgrown that it takes us almost an hour. By the time we reach them, we're both sweating. I offer Ceena my water skin and then take a swig when she's done.

"If nothing else, we at least know that no one else comes here." Ceena steps toward the cave entrance.

"For sure." I pull out my oil box and light it. "Let's do this."

As we enter the gloom, I'm glad for the illumination the oil box provides. From the dirt and debris littering the entrance, Ceena's right. We're the first people here in a long time. We stroll down the tunnel that leads to the open room and the various sub-tunnels at its end. When we reach the room, we stop. It's difficult to describe the awe that the drawings on the wall inspire.

By unspoken agreement, we approach the walls and examine the paintings. The enclave's history is recorded here for all to see and remember. I gaze at the numerous sections, associating them with various stories the council relates on different occasions. The stories painted on the wall more or less run chronologically, starting at one end of the room and then working their way around almost the entire area.

"I wonder that they used for paint," Ceena muses. "I'd love to get my hands on some. It would be wonderful to have colors that don't fade for my mats."

I'm about to answer, but I've reached the end of the line. Silently, I grab Ceena's arm and point at the wall. Together, we gaze at the scene: a group of men carrying what is undoubtedly the box we've brought with us. This picture shows the sapphires on the box, and I wonder again why that detail has been omitted in the tale's retelling. But my focus is more on what follows the scene of the men taking the box away and the close-up of the symbol on the box. Black ink billows from the box as it's dropped into a pool, drifting away from the box to the next scene, where the black swirls together into a savage spiral that dives to an all-black center.

The black is mesmerizing, drawing me in until I feel like my very soul is being wrenched from my body. I stumble backward, breaking the grip the image has on me and gasping for air. It's then that I notice Ceena still standing there, her eyes blank and glassy. I lurch forward and yank her away from the wall with its patch of black death.

Ceena sputters as she gulps down air. When she's finally able to breath, she says, "What was that?"

I shake my head, still rattled. "I have no idea. But don't look at it again."

"I agree." Ceena pants, still trying to get her breath back.

When she recovers, we study the side tunnels.

"Which one do you think?" I ask.

"They all look the same," Ceena observes, agreeing with what I've been thinking.

"Let's take the far one then."

We amble down the tunnel and are both pleasantly surprised when it extends further into the side of the mountain than we thought it was going to. Even better, it has several side tunnels of its own. Carefully, Ceena and I mark out a path, keeping track of our turns until we reach a branch that has plenty of natural alcoves at varying heights.

"I think we've reached the spot," I comment.

Ceena agrees, and we start checking out the various pockets until Ceena shouts, "This one!"

I cross to where she stands, indicating an alcove about a foot over her head. Since she's taller than most of the women in the enclave, it's a fair way up the wall. I step closer and run my hand into the opening. It runs further back than my fingers can.

"Let's give it a try," I say, retrieving the box and handing it to Ceena. She stares at it, uncomprehending. "I'm going to lift you so you can push it as far back as it will go." Only after I've said the words do I wonder whether she'll be okay with the idea.

But Ceena doesn't complain. Either she's more unnerved by our experience at the wall painting, or she understands the need to get the box back as far as possible. I cup my hands for her to stand on, and she puts a dainty foot into them. I try not to think of how close she is as I give her the boost needed to get her onto my shoulders. Her free hand resting on my shoulder as she swings around to wrap her legs over my shoulder does nothing to help me forget. For a moment I almost wish she weighed more as supporting a heavier burden would've given me something else to think about.

"Move a little closer," Ceena directs.

I oblige and feel her pressing against the back of my head as she leans forward to place the box in the opening.

"All done," she whispers. I reach up and support her arms as I help her down. I can't help thinking I'm glad the light is so dim because it means she can't see how flustered I am. I check that thought as I notice her staring at me.

Quickly, I turn away and head further away from the alcove.

"Aiken, where are you going?"

"I want to check that people coming into this tunnel can't see the box from a distance." Being the tallest person in the enclave means that if I can't see it from a distance, it's unlikely anyone else will be able to either.

"Well?" Ceena demands a few seconds later.

"Yeah, that spot's perfect. I can't see it and I'm looking for it."

"Time to head back then?"

I'm not sure, but I can almost swear there's a wistfulness to her voice. *What's that about?* Deciding I don't have time to dwell on it, I answer her question as though I didn't notice her tone.

"Yes. Hopefully the trip back won't take as long. Although we've probably been gone long enough for everyone to notice our absence already." Despite the dim light, I can see Ceena's going to argue about why we should hurry back if it's pointless. I cut her off before she can start. "Let's go."

I take off back down the tunnel toward the exit. I wonder if I'm going to have to stop when I don't hear her following. I'm about to give in when I hear her footsteps echoing my own. The trip back is completed in silence. I almost don't notice it because I'm so wrapped up in wondering why she wanted to linger. Perhaps I shouldn't have cut her off. If I'd let her finish, I would've learned more. *"There's nothing to be gained by being hasty."* One of the few things my father told me as a young boy returns to haunt me.

Whether it's because I'm so preoccupied or because we're more familiar with the route, I'm not sure, but we seem to reach the paths near the village quicker than on the trip out. I open my mouth to suggest to Ceena that we part ways when I hear the screaming.

CHAPTER NINE

The cries are awful. High-pitched, terrified, anguished. What could make many people cry out so vehemently? I dart a glance at Ceena. She gazes back, eyes wide and frightened. But there's a grim set to her jaw. She won't let anything get in the way of finding her brother. Without a word, we start sprinting. Breaking free of the forest, we are met with a sight almost too unbelievable to be true.

Smoke belches over the village in thick, dirty grey clouds. Like eels slithering through water, huge beasts ride the skies, sliding through the smoke. I squint, trying to make out what they are, but I've never seen creatures like this before. They have vicious beaks like raptors the tails of scorpions, wings with slashing blades at the end and talon-tipped claws. Every part of them is designed for delivering death. And they excel at it.

Aghast, I stare at the broken bodies of villagers strewn from one end of the field to the other. Blood stains their clothes bright red, seeping into the soil as the life drains out of them. I scan the faces, hoping for some sign of life, but I only find the empty eyes of too many friends. Where are the warriors?

They're not among the dead. The smoke blows clear of the village for an instant, and I notice an accumulation of the monsters there. In that moment, I know I've answered my own question. I barrel up the hill to the village entrance. I'm almost there when I realize Ceena's right behind me.

"What are you doing?" I yell over my shoulder.

"Finding Tamaan," she snaps.

Fair enough. She won't be dissuaded from that, but if I've learnt anything about Tamaan at all since we began training together, he's more worried about his sister than himself. "You do know he'll fight better and be safer if he knows you're alright?"

"Why do you think I'm tailing you?"

Apparently, I misjudged her motivation. "As long as you understand you should get to safety as soon as he sees you, we're good."

"I have no desire to get my brother killed by splitting his focus," Ceena grates.

Alright, I'll leave it at that. We hurtle toward the congregated monsters, a beacon for our destination. I choose the path that will take me past my home while avoiding the fires burning in several houses. It takes only a few seconds to dash inside and grab my weapons. By the time I'm outside again, Ceena's caught up to me.

We reach the village center. Blood spatters the walls, the ground, the warriors still standing, those already fallen. Its coppery stench assails my nostrils. The anger that was simmering just below the surface boils over and with a bellow, I join the fray.

Slashing at the nearest beast with my spear, I'm stunned to find the hide almost impenetrable. My spear only sinks in an inch or two. I shove harder, but the wooden shaft bends. Retracting the spear before it breaks, I stare at the monster. *How is this possible?*

It ducks its ugly head toward me, and I glide sideways to avoid the beak with its serrated, razor-sharp edges. I almost gag as I catch a whiff of its foul breath when the beak passes by, so close that it's impossible not to see the blood staining it. I'm so focused on the beak that I almost miss the talons that follow. I dive onto the dirt and roll away. Bouncing back up onto my feet, I begin strategizing.

"We can't gain ground," I hear someone shouting.

"Our weapons don't work on these beasts," I yell back. "Not unless they have a vulnerable spot. Anyone know where that is?"

"Between the scales on the neck," someone else hollers.

Recognizing Tamaan's voice, I'm amazed at the relief I feel. Hopefully Ceena heard him too. But there's no time for distractions. We need to find weapons that will be more effective against the armored hides of these mutants.

My eyes scan the immediate area. This is where we keep our livestock, so there's not much here. We determined long ago that raiders were more interested in food than anything else. By sequestering our livestock in several areas near the center of the village, we both reduced the number of animals we lost to raids and the number of raids launched against us once word got out about how secure our animals were.

My eyes are still roaming the area when I spot a discarded pitchfork. As a tail swipes at me, I dive to the side, then begin a zigzag path toward the pitchfork. I reach it just as another monster swoops down on me. Diving for the pitchfork, I snatch it up and roll onto my back. Supporting the base of the pitchfork against the ground, I lift the tines into the air.

The monster screeches, a shrill, earsplitting sound that almost makes me drop the pitchfork. I grit my teeth and tighten my hold. Just as well because the monster smashes into it. The force shuddering through the pitchfork reverberates all the way to my bones. Then hot, black liquid spurts from the monster, gushing over me. I gag again at the stench, twisting sideways to escape the muck.

Free, I stare at the beast. It's impaled on the pitchfork. The stuff shooting over me is obviously its mutated blood. The pitchfork penetrated the beast's hide. It's dead. These things *can* be killed.

"Pitchforks," I scream, but it comes out as a hoarse croak. I try again, this time succeeding. "Pitchforks!"

"What?" Tamaan yells.

I realize he's closest to me. "Tell everyone to use metal. Pitchforks, hoes, post diggers. They can pierce the hide."

Tamaan relays my instructions to those closest to him, who in turn pass the word on. Abruptly, men scatter in search of metal objects. I roll onto my feet, wiping the monster's blood off my face. I shove the dead beast so that it falls sideways and jerk the pitchfork out. *Time for payback. Time to avenge those who've been lost.*

It feels like hours later that I stand, watching, as the beasts finally retreat. In reality, it can't have been more than fifteen minutes. I'm covered in gore and have more than a few cuts evidencing my efforts. Mercifully, none of my injuries are severe. I take in those around me. Too many others aren't as fortunate. I make my way toward the closest fallen warrior and begin checking to see what can be done for his wounds, if anything.

Two hours later, I stagger to my feet again. My throat is raw, and my eyes burn from the smoke that still hangs in the air despite extinguishing the fires. As I rise, my eyes meet Ceena's. They surely reflect the horror and loss I'm feeling. But her tears ring warning bells. "What?"

"Racella, she didn't—" she begins before the sobs obscure her words.

Without a second thought, I wrap her in my arms. I don't care if she takes this the wrong way. I need the comfort of having her close as much as she needs me to comfort her. We stand there, taking solace in the warmth of contact with another living being. When emotion eventually breaks the barrier of numbness I've been subjected to since we first saw the attack, I know it's time to let her go.

"Time we see to the living," I say as gently as I can.

She nods, her eyes still brimming with tears and red from weeping. I admire her courage when she turns and begins seeing to the children wandering aimlessly around us. At least we were able to keep them safe. That was why all the warriors were in this area. Regrettably, at least half of these children will be in the situation I was in all those years ago when I lost both my parents on the same day.

"You saved me." The wonder in Malthasus's voice makes me turn, curious to see who he's addressing. Blow me down with a feather if it's not Tamaan. *Wow and double wow!* The boy overcame his resentment of Malthasus to do the right thing in battle.

Tamaan nods at Malthasus. "Well, you didn't have your spear."

I place a hand on Tamaan's shoulder. "Good man."

The grin he gives me is a reward on its own. I smile in return and notice the pride he feels straightening his spine and making him stand taller. Whether he knows it or not, he became a man today.

"Time to start rounding everyone up." As I turn to survey the people, I notice Malthasus scowling. He bestows a venomous glare on me before spinning and stomping off. *What's that's about?*

"Why?" Tamaan's question brings me back to the situation at hand.

"If those aberrations return, we have no means to protect the people." I gesture toward the ruined homes. "Do you know how the fires started?"

Tamaan shakes his head. "I was in the fields when they first arrived, so I didn't see. I heard some mutterings that they toppled the cook fires, then dropped clothes they'd snatched from the drying lines to make the flames spread faster. It all sounds a little unrealistic to me, and yet the evidence speaks for itself."

"I suppose how they did it is irrelevant in the grand scheme of things," I say. "Let's get these people focused on preparing for a trip."

"Where are we going?"

"I have a place in mind."

The sun has long set by the time our exhausted group approaches the caves Ceena and I left only this morning.

"This is a worthy place to begin rebuilding," Breiden says to me when we're in the large room on the far side of the entrance.

Personally, I'm glad he was one of the council members who survived because I like him. Maybe he likes me too because he's the one who convinced the other survivors to follow my advice about moving the enclave to a more defensible area.

I only nod agreement as the people shuffle in. Everyone's too tired to bother with exploring the maze of tunnels. Most people flop down within thirty feet of the opening and are asleep almost the moment they do. I dump my own things, along with the pitchforks I brought, at the part of the cave closest to the the tunnels. I briefly consider moving the box, but considering the state of those around me, I decide against it. I'll check on it in the morning.

But the moment I wake the next morning, I remember I didn't check my snares last night. It's the first time I've ever done this, and the thought of having left animals trapped overnight horrifies me. There's no time for anything except to get out there and clear those snares.

When I'm only partway finished, I realize I have more game than I can carry. I return to the caves to gather some youngsters to help me. *Probably good for them to have something to do*, I think as we traverse the forest collecting the game.

By the time we return, it's nearly noon. I'm heartened to see that whilst we were gone, cook fires have been set up. The people will eat tonight, and the process of rebuilding will begin.

As I enter the caves after delivering the meat, I find Breiden waiting for me. Malthasus stands next to him, his stance hostile and his face defiant. Next to them are the rest of the remaining council members. My stomach drops. Something is horribly wrong.

Breiden holds something out to me. "Where did you get this?"

I squint into the gloom, my eyes struggling to adjust after the bright sunshine outside. Then a blue glint catches my eye. And I know what he's holding. It's the cursed stone box!

CHAPTER TEN

My anger flares anew How could Malthasus have done that? No, a better question is how Malthasus thought that betraying Ceena and I to the council would help him win Ceena over? What was he thinking? Evidently, he wasn't. His desire for Ceena is clearly affecting his thinking.

Thumping the stone wall with the side of my fist, the blaze of pain does nothing to dull my irritation. *How did I not notice Malthasus following us when Ceena and I set off with the box?* I gouge the compacted soil with a fingernail, grinding away at it until my finger starts bleeding as I process what must've happened.

The only way for Malthasus to have followed us all the way to the caves was if he was with us from the beginning. Tracing things backward, he could only have done that if he started at Ceena's home. That's a disturbing thought. *Why was he there? Was he watching her? Perhaps hoping to catch her on her own? Only, I was there. And then Ceena left before I did, so he couldn't confront her then either.*

Malthasus must've followed Ceena to my home. No doubt what sparked his jealousy. When he saw Ceena meet up with me in the forest a few minutes later, that only made it worse. His pride wouldn't allow me to lead Ceena to some romantic spot, so he'd followed.

Except he must've heard enough of our conversation along the way to gather that we planned on hiding a box in the caves. Whether he knew it was "the" box, I don't know, because I can't recall whether we mentioned this fact while we talked.

Once Malthasus was satisfied this wasn't going to be a romantic liaison and that we would head back to the village as soon as our task was accomplished, he had to have hightailed it back to the village to get there before us. No wonder he didn't have his spear with him and Tamaan had to save him!

I suck my bleeding finger. With Racella gone, there's no pressing need for Ceena to attend the Festival with Malthasus. Especially now that he's probably realized Tamaan is a better fighter than Malthasus gave him credit for. I recall Malthasus's anger in the village and wonder if it's because he realized I've been training Tamaan. *Does he see this as a betrayal?* Not only am I training Tamaan, but in his eyes, I'm also standing between him and Ceena. An obstacle that has to be removed.

Malthasus must've started searching the caves as soon as we arrived. When he found the box, it didn't take him long to hand it over to the council, probably with some baloney about Ceena and I wanting to keep its treasures for ourselves. *His jealousy is making him crazy. Did he really think he'd be able to tarnish my reputation so easily?* If anything, it's only made the council more wary of him. His actions are not those of an honorable man. If he still thinks he'll get their blessing to marry Ceena, he's in for a rude awakening. Or at least I hope so.

Attempting to divert my thoughts from worrying about Ceena's fate, I study my improvised prison. It's a small cave at the end of one of the tunnels. Two guards are stationed outside; I hear the murmur of their voices as they speak in subdued tones.

Blast Malthasus and his wretched ego! Why does he always have to try and prove himself to everyone? Of course I know the reason why. He's never gotten over the shame of his birth or the fact that his father was not a member of the enclave. It only adds fuel to the fire for the situation I find myself in. I hope Ceena's in a better place than I am. And there I go again, my thoughts drifting back to Ceena. I sigh.

It must be an hour later when I hear a new voice join those at the end of the corridor. I perk up as footsteps head my way. I tense, unsure who to expect. I'm relieved when Breiden appears.

"What have you done with Ceena? She's not a part of this. You have to let her go," I begin before noticing that Breiden holds the stone box. "Why have you brought that here?"

"Which question should I answer first?" Breiden asks, amusement coloring his voice.

"Is Ceena alright?"

"She is. And no, she has not been detained as you were. Nor was she placed under guard. She is not the threat to us that you could potentially be."

"What?"

Breiden sighs. "Aiken, you're our best warrior. Don't think I don't know that you could've overcome those guards outside and escaped if you'd wanted to."

"Why on earth would I want to do that?" I roar, my frustration breaking the barrier of my self-control. The whole world has gone insane.

Instead of answering my question, Breiden says, "There are some things that you don't know about this box."

And there it is. The confirmation of my suspicions that the council doesn't always tell us everything. "Like what?"

"May I sit?" Breiden's tone is calm and I realize that I'm behaving like a moron. I motion for him to go ahead, remaining silent once he's seated cross-legged opposite me, waiting for the answer to my question.

Sighing, Breiden begins. "What we were ordered not to pass along with the tale is that the person who found this box would be the one to open it."

I snort. "You don't think I tried?"

Breiden proffers the box. "Try again."

I stare at the box, resenting that I ever found it. When I realize Breiden won't speak further or leave until I do, I snatch the box from his hands. *How does he expect me to open it?* Last time, I couldn't, no matter what I tried. I examine at the box, trying to find some sort of lock this time. There isn't one. Huffing, I dump the box in front of me. "Satisfied?"

To my immense aggravation, Breiden only smiles. "Have I ever told you about the time I had to fetch water for my mother the first time?"

Really? The world truly has gone insane. Why does Breiden want to tell me a story now? And such a benign one at that? Resigned, I shrug. Breiden launches into the tale. Two sentences in I already know this is going to bore me out of my skull. Wanting something to do, I pick up the box and begin tossing it from hand to hand, listening as the object inside rattles around.

Breiden's voice drones on, and I'm just thinking what a nice background noise it would be to fall asleep to when something gives as I catch the box. But my reflexes are faster than my brain, and I've already tossed the box again before I can stop myself. The box smashes into my other hand, and it gives a little more.

I tune Breiden out altogether as I examine the box. I can't see anything. I run my fingers down the corners of the box. Still nothing. I push on the gems, and that's when it happens: my fingers trace a pattern of their own accord. I'm so bewildered that I just let the rhythm play through my fingers. As I hit the last gem, there's a blinding flash of blue. The box falls apart. Whatever was inside falls to the floor.

I grope around for the mysterious object, since my eyes are still watering from the intense light. It's virtually impossible to see in the semi-darkness. Frustrated when my fingers find nothing, I leap to my feet and grab the torch off the wall. Dropping down to all fours, I lower the flame until it's almost touching the ground. The flat, white object shows itself.

Reaching forward, I touch it. It's about as long as my finger and feels like it's made from wood. On closer inspection, I notice several holes along one side. *A whistle? That's what all the fuss was about? A whistle?*

"Is this a joke?" I ask, rounding on Breiden. Before he opens his mouth to reply, I see the answer on his face. *Alrighty then, not a joke. But there must be some explanation for how my fingers knew which gems to push.* "How did I know how to open the box?"

Breiden shakes his head. "I know as much as you do."

I give him a pointed stare and raise my eyebrows.

"Okay, so I do know a little more, but only that you would be able to open it. Not how you would know to do so. Also, before you ask, yes, I also know that you're meant to use the item the box contains."

I stare at him for a moment, processing. "You mean I should blow the whistle?"

"Yes."

"But weren't you—or rather all the council—the ones who said this box would spell doom for our world?"

"We were. And if you had told us about finding the box when you did, perhaps we would've been more prepared for those monsters that attacked us."

"You think those monsters are going to be the cause of the end our world?"

Instead of answering, Breiden turns the table on me. "What do you think?"

"I guess it's possible."

We sit in silence for a few minutes before Breiden says, "Well, are you going to blow that whistle?"

We've got nothing to lose at this point. If the prophecy said I should use the item, I'm going to use it. Placing my mouth at one end, I blow as hard as I can. When there's no sound, I flip the reed around and blow on the other side. That doesn't work either. I frown. "Maybe it's broken?"

Breiden's eyes get a faraway look. "Perhaps." He stands. "Let's get you out of here. You need to run the evening check on your snares. And dinner's almost ready."

I gawk. "Really? No apology? No more recriminations for finding the box? Or breaking the whistle?"

Breiden smiles. "Sometimes all we need is a little time to figure things out."

With that cryptic sentence, he trudges back down the tunnel.

Deciding I'd rather be out in the forest checking my snares than here, I hurry after him. We're nearing the main entrance when we hear the shouts. *Not again,* I think as I sprint toward the sounds.

Barging through the people trying to escape further back into the cave, I burst out of the entrance just in time to catch the shadow of something enormous passing overhead. I charge back into the cave and grab a pitchfork from the pile I dumped on the floor last night. When I race back to the opening, Tamaan's right next to me.

I turn my attention back to the opening just in time to stop before I run into it. Standing there on short little legs is the oddest creature I've ever seen. It's feathered and shaped like an owl, but arms poke from its sides in addition to its wings. The furry ears, overly large eyes, and cute triangular ears standing straight up on the top of its head make it oddly appealing, but its predatory beak and the talons it has instead of feet give me pause. Best to exercise caution with this thing.

Unexpectedly, it takes a single hop towards me. I move my arm sideways, giving notice to the other warriors who have collected around me to take precautions but not to attack. The little thing stops and cocks its head as it studies me. Then it hops closer. I'm in two minds as to what to do when it stops less than five feet from me.

"Greetings, alarmed be not. Here to help we are," it says. Its voice is just as cuddly as its appearance.

I tell myself not to be swayed by its innocent appearance. "Who's 'we?'"

The trees behind him rustle as two gigantic creatures emerge. Gesturing towards them, the creature says, "This be 'we.'"

Trying to keep an eye on the fuzzball, I dart a quick glance at the beasts that are now fully revealed. I gasp. They look exactly like bats. Except for their size. These specimens are countless times the size of the ones I'm familiar with.

"Invite us in, will you not?" the fuzzball enquires.

I glance back at Breiden, now standing with the other council members gathered behind me. He nods.

"Sure, come on in. I'd like to hear how three of you are going to help with our problem," I say, not hiding my sarcasm.

"Oh, three of us there are not. Hundreds of us there are. Up there they stay. No place for them here there be," Fuzzball says, pointing upward.

I peer through the canopy of leaves. That's when I see them, just as it said. Hundreds of these giant bats, wheeling and circling overhead. *We're well and truly up the creek without a paddle if they're not here to help..*

CHAPTER ELEVEN

It's been an insane few weeks. Zareh, a.k.a. Fuzzball, spent that first night filling us in on the Gaptors' history. We gave the monsters the name "Gaptors" after the one Zareh supplied was impossible for us to pronounce. After much debate, we settled on a cross between "predator" and the "gap" those aberrations crossed between worlds to get to us. Essentially, the Gaptors have been at war with Zareh and his allies (including the giant bats known as gliders) for millennia.

Their last battle, epic by all accounts, almost culminated in the capture of their leader. As a result, he disappeared. Spies sent to find him never returned. Yet word somehow filtered back that he was planning an attack on another world.

In response, Zareh's leader sent emissaries through the breach with the stone box and its precious whistle. A whistle that could reach across realms to prevent our world—one sorely equipped to deal with Gaptors—from suffering the ravages of the Gaptor attacks. Our ancestors were given instructions regarding the box, and the emissaries left, hoping never to have to return to our world. Regrettably, that was a futile hope.

I still haven't wrapped my mind around these startling revelations: that they're all from another world; that the whistle I blew was placed here for the specific purpose of summoning them should there ever be a breach between our worlds; that they've all been alive for centuries, which was when that last famed battle happened.

The weeks since those revelations feel just as surreal. It's been a whirlwind of learning how to ride the backs of the gliders and them training us for aerial battles, all the while traveling to settlements near and far in search of more voyagers (the name given to those who ride on the backs of gliders). Finding volunteers for the fight wasn't difficult. Almost every settlement of note has been attacked. Every glider now has a voyager, and our small army is ready for the attack, according to Zareh's assessment.

We congregate in the fields around our village. We agreed this would be the staging ground for the battle, since our home is the best match for natural terrain that can take advantage of the Gaptors' weaknesses.

I glance at Ceena, standing next to her own glider. Shockingly, Zareh insisted nothing said only men could fight. Any who wanted to learn how to fight the invaders were welcome. More than a few warriors were speechless when several women stepped forward as volunteers. I can't say whether I was surprised when Ceena joined them, but I am amazed at how skilled she's become in such a short time. She displays the same natural abilities as her brother. Maybe it runs in their family.

My thoughts snap back when Zareh calls for everyone's attention. Our gliders take to the air so we can gather around Zareh. Using the firm sand next to the river bed, he outlines the proposed plan of attack. When he's finished speaking, he opens the floor for questions or comments, but no one takes him up on the offer. His plan is solid.

"The victors be then, your homes reclaim," Zareh says by way of dismissal.

Not quite what I would've said to rally the troops, but I suppose it'll do. I face Ceena, who opted to stand right next to me for Zareh's presentation. I wonder why she chose to do that. She knows she doesn't owe me anything. Tamaan, right behind her, lifts his chin to acknowledge me before drifting away to the area where gliders are swooping down to collect their voyagers.

My eyes meet Ceena's, and I wonder if she's scared. Her brown eyes are alive with anticipation, and there's a soft smile on those ruby lips. Her ebony hair frames her face perfectly—no stray hairs to tuck away today. Her hair is twisted into in a single long braid, perfect for battle.

My doubts about what I should do about how I feel about her surface for the umpteenth time. On the one hand, I would still really like her to be the one to give some indication that she accepts me for who I am and not what I can do for her. But the larger part of me can't help wondering whether this is the last time we'll ever be together.

Ceena steps toward me, and I step back, surprised. It must show because she says, "Why are you backing up?"

Flustered, I wave a hand in the air, fishing for words I can't find. Then, before I do, she closes the distance between us and pulls me into a hug. Her arms around me are strong and fierce, drawing me into her as though trying to absorb me. I'm savoring the contact when she drops her arms so suddenly, I can only stand there, stunned.

My words come in a rush. "What was that for?" My tone is harsher than I intended. Ceena blushes, and I feel terrible. But now is not the time for games. I need an answer.

Ceena ducks her head, casting her eyes down and then off to the side before she finally raises her chin, squares her shoulders, and looks me right in the eyes. "I like you Aiken Dartanus. And I want you to attend the Festival with me. So you'd better live through this fight."

My eyebrows shoot up. Then I can't hold back the grin. "And what are you going to do about it if I can't live up to that request?"

Her shoulders relax, and she giggles. "I'll chase after you and bring you back, no matter where you've gone."

A chuckle escapes me. *Yes, I believe she would.* Wonder and joy suffuse me, and I reach for her, tugging her back into my arms. This close, she smells like wildflowers and sweet beeswax. "Yes, I'll go the Festival with you. And to persuade you to live through this too—" I dip my head as I tilt Ceena's head gently upward with my thumb, "here's something to remind you what you have to live for."

I press my mouth to hers, kissing her tenderly. Her lips are soft, and I can't resist drawing her closer. Her strong, lithe body pressed against mine is heaven on earth. Her mouth tastes like honey. My senses swirl, and I want to extend the kiss, wanting every part of her, but I hold back, giving her the chance to pull back. When her arms snake around my neck, I smile against her mouth and deepen the kiss. It's only when I register the hoots and whistles in the background that I realize I've made this more intimate (and more public) than I should've.

Reluctantly, I draw back, memorizing her half-closed eyes, her dark lashes sweeping over them, her slightly parted mouth and flushed cheeks. She's never looked more beautiful. I don't let go just yet because I want to hold onto her forever. Her eyes open, and the heated liquid amber in them makes me want to kiss her again.

She smiles. "Oh yes, I'd like more of that. I'll do my best to stay alive."

Her first sentence bought ecstasy, the second sobriety. I sigh. It's time. "See that you do," I say as I release her.

The whistles and cat-calls have thankfully subsided, but Ceena doesn't seem to mind that I kissed her here in front of everyone. Grinning like a loon, I take her hand as we turn and stroll towards the pick-up area.

Minutes later, I'm swallowing my fear. Dread drops like a stone in the pit of my stomach as I watch Ceena aerial-connect with her glider. "Please, let her live." There's no more time for thought as my own glider descends.

Once in the air, we circle our fields, then aim for the forest. It seems small from this height. Then finally, we're past the forest and into the wasteland beyond. These canyons and mesas form the backbone of the caves our enclave currently uses as a home. *Who would've thought these magnificent mesas with their plunging cliffs and deep valleys would be the perfect place for an ambush?*

I glance at Tamaan on his glider next to me. We're both part of the group that volunteered to be the bait for this trap. What possessed us to make that decision, I have no idea, but here we are. I tighten my grip on my modified spear. Zareh personally supervised those who weren't training as they created new weapons for us. The shaft is hardened metal, the tip a shiny blade sharper than any I've ever carried. I wonder if Zareh used a special process to create these.

As our small group hovers, waiting for the Gaptors patrolling this area, I mull the events that led us here. From the moment Zareh arrived with his gliders, he took every precaution to ensure the Gaptors weren't alerted to their presence. When Zareh outlined the plan for today's attack, the reason became clear. The Gaptors had suffered such a crushing defeat in that last battle on their world that seeing any glider since then has sent them into an extermination frenzy. They will attack without regard for their own safety and, more importantly, without consulting their master. This is crucial to our success because the Gaptors aren't known for their mental acuity.

It's what we're relying on as we drift through their patrol area; that the patrolling group will spot us and give chase. Then, when we've ambushed that first group, the Gaptors will send subsequent patrols to investigate. We'll deal with them in the same way until we've obliterated them from the face of our world.

My hands start sweating as the minutes pass. Waiting is the worst part of battle. I'm all too aware of Zareh's warning that when the Gaptors take the bait, it'll be an insane race back to the ambush area. I'm beginning to wonder if this is going to be a long wait when there's a shout from someone near the back of the group.

I turn on my glider's back and see them: a group of five Gaptors headed our way. I rub the sweat from my palms and grip the fur on my glider's neck more firmly as we wait for the Gaptors to get closer as Zareh instructed us to do.

When they're less than fifty yards away, our small group turns and speeds away. We aren't prepared for the six Gaptors that we run into just on the other side of the bend in the valley. Yelling a warning to those following me, I tighten my knees around Terkus, my glider, as he dives down under the waiting Gaptors.

Pushing my body flat against Terkus's back as I've been taught, the pressure on my body eases. I position my spear for the loop he's about to take me on. My body strains as Terkus whips us back up into the swirling arc that will take us back over the waiting Gaptors. Then he plummets like a stone off a cliff as they pass under us.

As the first startled Gaptor appears beneath me, I drive my spear into its head. There's no sound as it dies and plunges downward, crashing into the Gaptor below it. This causes a problem for Terkus as there are now suddenly two obstacles blocking our downward trajectory.

In a nanosecond, Terkus snaps his wings tight, securing me as he spirals down between the two falling Gaptors. My head spins. Bile rises in my throat. *Humans definitely weren't made for flying*, I think as black spots dance before my eyes. I must be on the verge of passing out when Terkus abruptly opens his wings and zooms out of the spiral.

Choking back the bile, I shake my head trying to clear it.

"Spear!" Terkus shouts.

Instinctively, I raise my spear, and I'm almost knocked off Terkus as it connects with something. The Gaptor gives an otherworldly shriek and veers away, its one wing almost completely sheared off. I'm still trying to regain my balance when I notice two of the Gaptors racing away from our group.

"After them!" I holler.

If they escape, they'll ruin our plan. Terkus dials up the speed, but they have a significant head start. And although gliders are faster than Gaptors, this only holds true over short distances. I'm more than disappointed when we start falling further back after initially gaining on them.

"Come on, Terkus, we can do this!" I urge, anxious not to lose the minuscule advantage we have.

Terkus merely grunts as he pushes himself. Less than five minutes later, we have to concede defeat as the Gaptors vanish. To show appreciation, I rub Terkus's neck where I know he enjoys it the most. "Let's get back to the others."

Terkus hums softly under me, acknowledging the praise. Then he glides us around and back toward the others. When we reach them, I'm dismayed to notice we've already lost one pair of fighters. Although the fallen man is not from our village, his loss is nonetheless felt. Dealing with his remains will have to wait until this is over. I scan the area. While Terkus and I were chasing the fleeing Gaptors, the others took out not only the group that was waiting for us but also those who were following.

Which means we're back to waiting. Just as well, because I think Terkus could do with the rest. I study each of the other pairs in turn, relieved to find there aren't any serious injuries. A few cuts and scrapes, but not bad for our first skirmish.

The sound of rushing air draws my attention. I crush the fear that flares when I establish the cause. Gaptors headed our way. Too many to count. A black mass, covering the sky from one end to the other. *Well, I guess those two escapees got word to the others, and now they're here to avenge their brothers. Time to get on with it.*

CHAPTER TWELVE

As before, we wait until the Gaptors are about fifty yards away before commencing our mad charge to the ambush area. The scouts patrolling since the last attack assure us there aren't any more nasty surprises waiting for us.

We zoom down the valley toward the bend. Air rushes past me, my head pounds and the thirst for battle pulses in my veins. It's been a long time since I've felt this exhilarated and fearful simultaneously. *A good reminder that I'm alive—and that I'd like to stay that way.*

Rounding the bend, we race through the ever-narrowing ravine to the cliffs terminating this valley. *Do the Gaptors chasing us even wonder why we're not avoiding this route?* Obviously, the only reason we keep going is because there's a trap at the end. But as Zareh said, the Gaptors can only think of their desire for revenge. Any common sense they may have had has been overridden.

I count the seconds as we approach the end of the valley. Then we cross the imaginary line that will set the ambush in motion. As Terkus arcs down into the very bottom of the valley, the others in the group follow. Then pandemonium erupts. The bulk of the voyagers and their gliders that were hidden just beyond the edge of the steep cliffs bonding the ravine have descended on the unsuspecting Gaptors.

As soon as we hear the Gaptors' panicked squawks, Terkus twists under the pursuing Gaptors. Trapped between two lines of gliders, the Gaptors have nowhere to go. Frantic, they break ranks, desperate to escape the spears raining fatal strikes from above and beneath.

Their frenzied efforts only cause more chaos as they crash into one another. Some of them get their odd, spindly wings hopelessly entangled and crash to their deaths on the valley floor below.

Despite our terrible odds against so many Gaptors, Zareh's plan works flawlessly. The battle is bloody but brief. I gave up counting how many of the monsters I run through when I hit ten. After that, too many came too fast, and telling whether the blows I landed were fatal or not became impossible.

Now, Terkus and I float above the carnage beneath us. Gaptors lie dead and dying on the valley floor. Our team hasn't escaped unscathed either, but thankfully our losses are minimal compared to what they could've been had we faced these creatures in the open air. The slaughter would've been on our side for sure.

Weary, I shift my position on Terkus so I can survey what's behind us. After that first attempt at luring their patrol into a trap and finding we were the ones trapped instead, I am wary of accepting that things are truly over. Movement at the end of the valley draws my attention.

I squint, trying to make out what's moving against the dark edges of the cliffs. Terkus must've noticed that my attention was elsewhere because his gaze shifts in the same direction. His unexpected yell almost makes me lose my grip on him. "Gaptor on the horizon!"

As though expecting that I had seen it too, Terkus streaks forward, and I'm almost thrown off his back. Cursing, I inch back into position using his fur for leverage and then slam my legs down between his neck and shoulders, clamping tight as soon as I can.

"Can you hold on next time?" Terkus spits between clenched teeth. "Having my fur pulled like that is not the most pleasant experience!"

I grit my own teeth. "Well, if you'd remember that my eyesight isn't as good as yours, perhaps next time you'll provide a warning before taking off like that."

His annoyed grunt is his only answer as he picks up his pace. I realize Tamaan and his glider have joined us, as well as two other pairs I don't know. The eight of us give chase. As we close in on what turns out to be a lone Gaptor, I notice its lack of injuries. Either he escaped when we first attacked, or he was never part of the battle.

Pressing close to Terkus's ear, I urge him on. The dash of speed takes my breath away, but it serves the purpose. The Gaptor is within reach of my spear. Desperate to wound him before he can escape, I foolishly hurl my spear at him. Either he expected this, or he has incredible reflexes. The Gaptor tilts his strange wings ever so slightly, and my spear sails past. Before I can curse the lack of impact, the Gaptor turns on us. It's then that my folly is fully revealed. Terkus and I have set ourselves apart from the others. And I just tossed the only weapon I had.

Terkus dips his own wings to avoid the waiting Gaptor, and I duck down as the tail slashes towards my head when the Gaptor somersaults over us. This surprising tactic puts his beak right in line with my leg. The pain as the razor-sharp edge slices into my left leg is excruciating. I scream and clutch at my leg. Warm blood gushes past my fingers, the volume alarming.

If Terkus didn't rake the Gaptor's chest with his talons, I would've lost the leg altogether. The Gaptor screeches as it rears back and drops below us. Already, I can feel my strength ebbing as the blood loss continues unabated. Vaguely, I hear shouts and register that the others have caught up. I blink blearily as I try to find the Gaptor. It's gained on us again.

The chase wears on, and groggily, I think this Gaptor couldn't have been in the battle because it only picks up speed as our gliders begin to lag behind. Already battle weary, our gliders have nothing left to give as the Gaptor slowly pulls away from us. When it disappears from view, I expect we'll stop the chase. However, Terkus and the other gliders persevere. It's only when the Gaptor eludes even their vision that they relent.

For the second time today, Terkus and I have to accept that we just couldn't hack it. I'm too drained and despondent to bother bolstering

Terkus's spirits. It's no shocker he's in the same glum mood, and we limp back to the valley where the rest of the gliders wait.

By the time we get there, I'm feel faint from blood loss. As Terkus slides down to drop me off, I notice a crowd has gathered. At its center is Zareh.

That's the last I remember until I come around with a jolt. It's like someone threw ice water over me. I gasp and struggle up, trying to work out what just happened. I must've passed out. I reach out to grab at my leg, then stop in awe. There's no sign of the wound that could've ended my life. But the myriad of other cuts on my arms and torso are still there. They ache dully, reminding me to take it slow. *How is it my leg is healed but the rest of me isn't?*

I notice Zareh moving away from me. I was supposed to tell him something. In a rush, it floods back. Opening my mouth to call after him, the words die. As I watch, Zareh waves his hand over the injured people lined up on the ground before him. Cuts heal, broken bones mend, and sallow skin assumes a healthy glow once more. I'm too stunned to do anything except gawk. But I do understand now why I still have my other cuts: Zareh is only healing the most dire injuries. I have no idea how much time passes before Zareh heals the last person.

Spontaneous cheering erupts from those assembled. Zareh only nods that cute head of his, then waves everyone away. No one leaves. But Zareh must've sent some unseen signal, because the two massive gliders that accompanied him when he first arrived descend, driving the people clustered around him away with their enormous wings. Then they land and take up positions on either side of him, their wings forming a protective shelter around Zareh.

Through the arch in their wings, I see Zareh beckoning me. Uncertain, I rise and edge closer. I'm dumbfounded when the glider blocking my path drops a wing so I can enter the tight circle beyond.

"News for me, you have?" Zareh asks.

I drop my head. "I'm sorry, we weren't able to destroy that last Gaptor."

Zareh puts a tiny finger on his chin as he processes the information. "This to my compatriots, relay I must. Inform the villagers you will that return I shall."

I'm still deciphering his sentence when he vanishes. I blink. But no, the space in front of me is still vacant. I peer around the wings encircling me. But there's no sign of Zareh. I cringe as the gliders next to me abruptly launch themselves into the air. With a few strokes of their powerful wings, they're gone.

Dazed, I stand there until I feel a hand on my shoulder. I turn and find Ceena's worried brown eyes studying me. The relief I feel that she is safe is too much. Without a word, I pull her into my arms and press her against me. The warmth of her body drives some of the chill from me. She seems to understand that no words are needed. Placing her head on my shoulder, she wraps her arms around me, and something surges in me. There is hope in this world. We just have to find it and grab onto it.

Ten days later, I'm struggling to hold onto that hope. Zareh told me to tell the people that he would be back. But there's still no sign of him even though the gliders remain near.

I survey the activity around me. It's almost unbelievable that ten days ago our home was a pile of rubble and ashes. From the moment Zareh left, our people have been hard at work, rebuilding what was lost in that first attack. Partially resurrected homes surround me, the forest rings with the sound of trees being felled, and children scamper about carting building supplies.

That's not all they carry. Some are loaded down with bright ribbons or food, all gathered at the last minute so we could celebrate properly. Tonight is the Harvest Festival. Despite the usual euphoria this event invokes, the villagers move with solemn faces as they go about their preparations. Even knowing Ceena will be attending with me tonight is not enough to pull me free of the desperation I'm feeling. *What if Zareh doesn't come back? What if the Gaptors return? How will our enclave survive long term if this threat isn't annulled?*

Squashing my worries, I take refuge in the forest. As I finish my evening check of the snares, my mind is too preoccupied for me to notice where my feet lead me. Only when I see the glittering water do I wrest myself from my stupor.

CHAPTER THIRTEEN

I stare at the pool. There's no doubt this is where I found the stone box. *What is the significance of it appearing again?* I start forward, then stop myself. *No, the last time I did this, I fell in. Or was pulled in.* That part's still unclear in my mind. The voice next me almost sends me into the pool again as I leap away, alarmed. My brain catches up, and I realize it's Zareh.

"Pardon?" I say, aware I didn't catch what he'd said.

"Glad you came, am I," Zareh repeats.

"I could say the same thing about you," I mutter.

"What by that do you imply?"

"You've taken your sweet time getting back here."

Zareh cocks his head as he studies me. Deciding to ignore the jibe, he says, "A gift for you, have I."

"If it's something like that stone box, no thanks!"

"More useful I think this you will find," Zareh chirps.

Well, the fuzzball has my attention. I wait. If he wants me to say something, he'll be here a long time.

Zareh waves his arms over me. I'm not sure how he does that as he's significantly shorter than me. That thought is blown away as the strangest sensation courses through my body. Heat trickles up from the tips of my feet, through my legs and up into my torso and arms. By the time it reaches my neck, it's an inferno streaking through me. I struggle for breath as the the fire burns up through my neck and then explodes inside my head. Blackness engulfs me.

When I come around, Zareh is sitting on a nearby log, watching me. *How dare he look so smug!* "What did you do to me?"

"For yourself, see," Zareh commands.

I have no clue what he means. As I put a hand out to push myself off the ground, it brushes against a tiny plant. I stare at the plant, realizing it will be useful for the aches that plague Breiden when it gets cold. Then I notice my arm.

I do a double-take. The cuts that were there and only just beginning to heal are completely gone. Quickly, I examine the rest of my body. *Yes, they're all gone.* I stare up at Zareh. "That's what it feels like when you heal people? That flame?"

Zareh smiles. "Welcome, you are."

I realize I haven't thanked him for healing me. Before I can rectify that, he continues. "But no. The flame the gift be, that upon you I have placed."

I'm confused. "What are you talking about?"

"The plant, its uses you knew when against it your hand rubbed?"

How did he know that? More importantly, how do I suddenly have that knowledge? I've never known how to use plants for medicinal purposes before. Thoughts bash around in my head until they coalesce into reason. "You've given me the ability to heal people?"

"That we have," Zareh chortles rubbing his hand together in glee. "As the finder of the stone box, this special gift on you we bestow. But this a secret is, which by your family must be kept. As reason for healing, the plants give. This gift, to your children pass. For come the time may when this skill again needed will be."

What? Seriously . . . what? My brain struggles to decode his curiously phrased sentences. Maybe I hit my head when I passed out, because I'm having serious difficulty time working out what he means.

Zareh reaches out a hand. "Come, the others we must call on. Not long it is before once again leave I must."

Dazed, I allow Zareh to help me up, wondering how he does that. Perhaps he's stronger than he looks—or he just uses magic to do what his height limitations won't allow. It's only when we reach the outskirts of the village that I understand who it is he meant to call on.

The scouts spot Zareh, and the call goes up. I smile as villagers rush out, eager to see Zareh for themselves. I scan the faces. Malthasus's is still missing. Ever since the ambush, no one's seen him. He hasn't turned up in any of the nearby villages. His body wasn't among those recovered after the battle. And while it's possible his body may have fallen into an inaccessible area during the battle, I doubt it. More likely, Malthasus ran.

Few people know that shortly before the battle, the council informed Malthasus that he would be the subject of a tribunal when life returned to normal. Apparently, they decided a more formal setting was required to address the false allegations he made against Ceena and I. I'm not surprised, as this isn't the first time he's been caught in a lie. Take this in addition to the fact that he wasn't exactly known for facing situations where the odds were stacked against him —as they were when we faced so many Gaptors with so few gliders. These factors together convince me he's chosen to hide from his actions rather than face them.

I sigh inwardly. Hopefully, wherever he is, he will learn that he can't run forever. The upside of him being gone is that I no longer have to worry about Ceena's safety. A boon to be thankful for, without doubt.

The buzzing crowd pulls me back to the present. From the mix of emotions on their faces at the sight of Zareh, I know tonight's celebration will be one for the record books.

I'm not wrong. Zareh's arrival is the catalyst needed to get the celebrations underway. Those roasting the meat pick up their carving knives, people scatter for their plates, musicians take up their instruments, and children sidle to the tables to stuff as many sweet treats into their mouths as they can before the adults chase them away.

I don't wait around to observe the rest of the start of the festivities. Instead, I dump my evening catch with the cooks, then sneak down to the river to bathe. If I'm dancing with Ceena tonight, the last thing I want is to smell like the game I caught.

An hour later, I'm standing on the fringes of those gathered, searching for Ceena. When I see her, my heart bumps in my chest. She's breathtaking, wearing a sunflower yellow dress I've never seen before. It accentuates her dark hair, honey-toned skin, and amazing lips perfectly. Her hair is swept up into an intricate braid, the tiny beads woven into them sparkling as they catch the light from the nearby fires. She spots me and smiles, the most glorious thing I've seen in days. I can't help staring as she glides through the crowds towards me.

Suddenly unable to wait for her to reach me, I ease into the swell of people and cut a line toward her. We meet in the middle of the dance floor. For a moment, we only gaze at each other. Then I sweep her into my arms. I drop my head close to her ear and whisper, "You look stunning!"

She giggles and replies, "You don't look half bad yourself."

Her soft body pressed against mine again is a luxury I haven't allowed myself to think of since the day of our retribution against our enemies. Although we've tried to single out "alone time" in the last ten days, it's as though fate was intervening at every step. If I wasn't out gathering the fruits of my labor, she was being summoned by the village women to aid them with weaving new blankets and clothes to replace what was lost. Since her home was one of the few to survive the attack, her mats and baskets have also been in demand, and she's had to work out a system of loans instead of purchases to cope with it.

Now, finally, we're together. I relish her closeness. It seems she's doing likewise as she makes no effort to move away to a more appropriate distance for those not yet married. Then again, I don't really care what's generally accepted anymore. Life is too short and too full of unexpected twists to not take full advantage of what's right in front of us right now. With that in mind, I dip my head towards hers, intending to kiss her.

Abruptly, the crowd hushes. My head snaps up, and I scan for danger, relaxing when I realize Zareh is to blame. Turning Ceena in my arms so that she faces Zareh, I cradle her against my chest, loathe to release her.

Zareh dips his head at the crowd. "Excel you have at the task you were given. Grateful to you, those from our world are." Turning to one of his massive bodyguards, the glider presents a large bag. Zareh takes the bag and reaches inside. "Gifts for you, brought I have." He retrieves a small, roundish object. "Medallions these are, for your protection intended. Keep them safe you must. From generation to generation pass. For come the day will, when once again work together we may."

He continues to hand out instructions as he passes the bag to the first council member and indicates the bag should be passed along until one member of each family has a medallion. I can't say I'm surprised when there's the exact number of medallions for the families in our village.

Fingering my medallion, I admire its intricate design and beauty. *Is it relevant that this medallion bears the same symbol as the stone box?* Deciding it's not important, I listen as Zareh doles out a long list of decrees concerning the medallions. My mind is beginning to haze when I realize he's stopped talking.

I rouse my attention in time to register that Zareh and the gliders are bidding us farewell. Before we can object, they've taken to the air, fast disappearing from sight. Stunned, we watch until their group vanishes from view. Silence reigns for about a second. Then everyone starts talking at once, discussing the medallions and the orders and the sudden departure of our allies.

My eyes find Ceena's. Without a word, we sneak off. Personally, I have no interest in these discussions. I can only think of Ceena. We've spent enough time apart.

We make for the forest, and I lead her to the area I used for training Tamaan, secure in the knowledge that he's the only other person in our enclave who knows of its existence. As the moonlight spills through the tree branches overhead, I draw Ceena into my arms.

There's no time like the present, and I intend to make the most of it. Our lips meet, and our bodies entwine. The kiss leaves both of us breathless. We pull apart, our smiles equally broad.

I know where my immediate future lies. My destiny has been set. Whatever may come, we will face it together.

* * *

Love short stories? Get *Forecast of Shadows* now!

ALSO BY BRONWYN LEROUX

Aww, Aiken and Ceena got their happy ending! But is this really the end of the Gaptors? Find out in the full-length complete series! Pick up *Dawn of Dreams*, the next book in the *Destiny* series.

Enjoy short reads? If you like jungle-law dystopian worlds, a woman with grit and some hard-hitting punches, then this book is for you! Get *Forecast of Shadows* now!

Books by Bronwyn Leroux:

Breach (A *Destiny* companion novella -this book)

Dawn of Dreams (*Destiny*, Book 1)

Dogs of Doom (*Destiny*, Book 2)

Doors of Destiny (*Destiny*, Book 3)

Duel of Death (*Destiny*, Book 4)

Forecast of Shadows

IF YOU ENJOYED THIS BOOK . . .

I would love it if you would please share it!

Reviews are the fairy dust that keep my wheels turning, thinking up fresh and exciting books for you - and they help other readers just like you discover new books to enjoy.

You can leave a review at https://bronwynleroux.com/BreachReview

GET THE NEXT BOOK IN THIS SERIES FREE

Interacting with my readers and building friendships is the most rewarding part of writing. I occasionally send newsletters with details on new releases, special offers and other bits of news you may find noteworthy. If you are interested in writing your own book, you can opt in for the additional bonus of weekly writing tips.

Enjoy these wonderful benefits, including your free book, by signing up at https://bronwynleroux.com/FreeDawn

Dedicated to aspiring writers everywhere

ABOUT THE AUTHOR

Born near the famed gold mines of South Africa (where dwarves are sure to prowl), it was the perfect place for Bronwyn to begin her adventures. They took her to another province, her Prince Charming and finally, half a world away to the dark palace of San Francisco. While the majestic Golden Gate Bridge and its Bay views were spectacular, the magical pull of the Colorado Rockies was irresistible. Bronwyn's family set off to explore yet again. Finding a sanctuary at last, this is Bronwyn's perfect place to create alternative universes. Here, her mind can roam and explore and she can conjure up fantastical books for young adults.

facebook.com/AuthorBronwynLeroux
twitter.com/bronwyn_leroux
instagram.com/bronwyn.leroux

www.ingramcontent.com/pod-product-compliance
Lightning Source LLC
Chambersburg PA
CBHW020142150626
46552CB00021B/1274